Eskimo Calling?

Jodie Jones

authorHOUSE®

AuthorHouse™ UK Ltd.
500 Avebury Boulevard
Central Milton Keynes, MK9 2BE
www.authorhouse.co.uk
Phone: 08001974150

© 2010 Jodie Jones. All rights reserved.

No part of this book may be reproduced, stored in a retrieval system, or transmitted by any means without the written permission of the author.

First published by AuthorHouse 1/13/2010

ISBN: 978-1-4490-5422-9 (sc)

This book is printed on acid-free paper.

TO MY SISTER - *apparently!!*

Javea 2009:
Beth - "Oh this book is dedicated to her sister!"
Mum - "Ahh well if you ever write a book then..."

BETH - A BEST FRIEND DISGUISED AS A SISTER - X

ONE

We were meeting on the steps near the shopping arcade between Victoria Coach and Victoria Train Station, that in itself brought back memories of stolen weekends years before.

I was pleased the weather had enabled sunglasses, a barrier for my eyes to search for him and see him all over before our eyes actually met.

Expectations had started with texts on my journey down. I love texts, though not whilst I was driving so they had been rushed. How can you be so uninhibited texting words to people that you would never actually say to them? Thankfully this had suited me fine because what I wanted and what I dare say were two very different things.

I had been worried about this meet more than any of our others throughout the last decade and before. It had been the longest time since we had met and a lot of things had changed. Had he changed? I hoped not. He again had become my waking thought as he did normally every couple of years, though this time it had been six. Nothing is normally as good as you want it to be. My mum always used to say that you enjoy yourself more at parties you didn't want to go to than the ones you get excited about. She was right of course, mums were, expectations usually spoilt everything. Everything except him. He had always lived up to expectations and most of the time surpassed them. He was something special and, thankfully he wasn't one of those guys who knew it. A cross between a natural beauty and some sparkle he was stunning and sent me into a tizz when we met at 18 and I expected he still would now at the age of 30.

> *Me eskimo calling?* hows this gonna go?
> *Him* howd u want it 2 go?
> *Me* honestly...?
> *Him* totally!!!
> *Me* I wanna meet how we used 2. the tingling excitement as I arrive at the meet point, the anticipation, the scariness of not impressing then it all heightening with one flash of your electric smile and it all disappearing with the brush of our lips...?!!

It was very 'teenage crush' talk but that's exactly how this, now man, made me feel. Besides, I thought, I should get the intention out there to stop the hours of nervousness and awkward being. When no reply arrived on my mobile, I wished I hadn't!

Looking down I somewhat regretted the bag I had packed for a simple one night city break. It was truly 'Stacey-esk' when she goes to meet Gavin for the first time in Leicester Square. I had to have Everything - *just in case* - isn't that the way? I would have to get rid of it before we grabbed a coffee, a beer, *each other*?!!

I perched one cheek on the stone wall and took out my mobile, desperate to see if I had a reply. I didn't, I'd ruined it all. Maybe all this luggage would stay packed and I'd go home an hour after arriving...

"Eskimo Calling?" said a familiar voice and I swung my head and its white blonde hair in its direction.

He walked up the steps towards me in my mind it was in slow motion. Over the years he had had many talents but time bending wasn't one of them. He was just mesmerising. The horrid smog stained buildings surrounding the steps and the bustle of tourists lost in our city melted away. He was here, with me, again, *finally*.

Dressed in jeans and a simple navy tee that matched his eyes. He was about four inch's bigger than my 5ft 6" frame but that always allowed me to wear heels - another positive in his favour! His body wasn't rippling nor was it school boyish. It had always just been good. No over rated six pack just a slightly hard chest and slim build. His shoulders were perhaps a bit bulkier than the usual 30 year old man but I never knew how a solicitor kept them!

With one swift movement he had removed my safety barrier sunglasses and entwined his fingers between mine. Warm soft skin close to me, the tingling started. Every women knows how that feels. Deep in your tummy like a warm ache. It can make you do stupid things or loose the use of speech but none of us would change it. That feeling of excitement, anticipation, knowing you won't get a good nights sleep until you've tasted its cause. This daring nervous angst would stay whenever this man was around me.

As our eyes met and skin touched for the first time in years he said to me, 'Fancy building an igloo?'

I allowed myself to reminisce.

"Hey" he had said.

I jumped, how rude to expect me to wait for him to go down the stairs first. I looked up to fight my feminist corner but met his eyes. They were deep and sparkled when he smiled. A full, teeth bearing smile, his plump lips moist, inviting me in. I had been staring at them, and him, since arriving on this Arctic Experience trip with college four days previous. It was the escape from home I wanted not the walk through an Eskimos world as the brochure had suggested that had found me here. Despite what was starting to feel like endless days here I couldn't tell you what Eskimo's ate, how they survived or where they were but I could tell you what he had worn since he arrived. I guess I'll never know what I missed about the Eskimos that day or the next two but I figured I had a whole lifetime to get to know my own 'Eskimo'.

"Do you know where the TV lounge is?" *yumm his accent,* he asked.

"I...er...", The *'feeling'* took a hold. What a bizarre question, had I got this gorgeous stranger wrong? Was he really asking me directions?

As I failed to pronounce another sentence he grabbed my hand, laughing and pulled me into a room. Was I really going to come across as some bubbling teenager when in fact I was a competent, happy 18 year old with a crush that I had not felt since Mark Owen graced my walls.

In the dim light I could see a few sofas, tables. There was a slight glow from an old TV in the corner, *ahhh the TV lounge*? I could see enough to see him walk towards it, fiddle with the channels and begin to wonder towards me. I opened my mouth, I didn't know if it was to scream, confess my love or bark but damn it, words still weren't coming out of me. I stumbled backwards. My shoes squeaking on the flooring which like the rest of this place was cold and old. I could see my breath as my mind confronted the situation. What was I doing, forget me, what was *he* doing?

He got closer and closer. I pushed my hand out for the door handle but he got to me first. I should have been terrified in a dark room with a stranger but when he cupped my face in his hands, smiled that smile and gently and softly brushed his amazing lips onto mine I couldn't help but respond.

It started slow, long pouting touches of our mouths then longer open explorations as we explored with our tongues and I got to know his kisses.

My back found the cold door as our kisses got hungrier and our hands began to find new resting places. My hands wondered towards his lower back, past his belt line and below to a solid round behind. I must have stopped kissing when I found my new discovery as I hummed happily and he took my new drug - his lips - away. I laughed and slapped him playfully. I took in his aftershave, Polo Sport, as he hugged me and breathed onto my neck. My sides tingled and as I re-perched my hands on his wonderfully tempting derriere, the door knob turned into my lower back.

Shit - someone was coming in. I had visions of it being my tutor and being sent home for unreasonable behaviour with a stranger. Truth was it was my first any behaviour with a stranger and I didn't fancy explaining to mum the reason for my early return was 'a tingly feeling'.

Phew, thankfully my weight against it had made the intruders think the room was locked and we were again left to ourselves, in a darkened room with only the light of an Eskimo documentary muting away in the corner.

Seeing him again now had been nearly everything I'd asked for - *nearly*. I don't remember how we left the steps minutes before. I only ever think of the here and now when I am around this man. How else could I explain my thoughtless decision over the years and now. The busy rushing people were pushing us closer together and he hadn't let go of my hand since he entwined our fingers within moments of seeing me. He had the power to make me feeling a million dollars even with all these new strangers around I only saw him and I hoped he only saw me. He gave that impression, looking back occasionally as someone jumped into the door way before me or pushed me aside to make whatever their hurry was for. London had been a well chosen location to meet but I forgotten about all the others that would form part of our day.

As we grabbed a coffee at one of the many cafes lining the entrance to Victoria. It was funky with leather seating and snazzy lighting like most of them do now, even McDonalds have this generic smooth feel now. The smell made me chose a large Mocha even with this heat and carrot cake was a must whenever it was available. We caught up, laughed and joked. We easily slipped back into banter and back chat. The conversation flowed as it always has, carefully and flirty. He could have been talking about the Congo or aliens, neither of which I care for particularly, but my eyes didn't leave his lips. Occasionally he would touch them with a blink of concern, then I am sure, as he licked them moist he watched my eyes widen. God this man oozed appeal through every pore.

"What's all that?" His eyes caught sight of my oversized bag and I braced myself for the onslaught of ridicule I knew was coming. "You here for one night or seven!" he commented surprisingly subtly. Then I noticed him hunch his shoulder over and I caught sight of his record bag and smiled back to his winking yet smirking face.

I gulped down my coffee, *oh ow still hot.* "I'll drop it off at the hotel, its not far, a few stops on the central line." *add milk, ahh yes much cooler,* "I'll run over now if you want to wait around. Have I got you this afternoon or just now and dinner later?"

I got up, not waiting for his answer. I assumed he wouldn't follow me when he could just stay here for 30 minutes drinking expensive flavoured coffee and eating cake like I would given the choice. I turned to pick up my case and looked towards the exit. I went to walk forward but my step was lost as he swung for my arm and spun me around into him.

He grinned "You've got me as long as you want me!"

Our embrace was central for all to see. He tasted as good as I had remembered. Right there I was on cloud nine not a Victoria station cafe. His lips were still as additive. They still greeted me slowly, remembering each other and finding one another's depths again. It had been too long since I had kissed this man. By god I would make up for that. The longing in my stomach stretched away into bubbling exciting intrigue. He rolled his tongue with mine and I had to remind myself where we were. Now this reunion was Everything I had hoped it would be.

I stopped smooching as my conscious heard our coffee cups being cleared away and a young waitress mumbling something about not wanting anymore of the cake now I had found something equally as tasty to eat! How rude, *how true!*

I wiped my throbbing mouth, his stubble had sanded my lip line. "So hotel then?" I asked "Oh god, no. I meant to get rid of my suitcase, not err...". The waitress sniggered.

He kissed my embarrassment away and we walked to the tube entrance holding hands.

The tube journey flew by. I was lost in teenage giggles and secret touches of this equally thirty year old something who was touching back. I couldn't take my eyes off him. My barriers were down and I was totally at his mercy.

We entered the hotel and I wondered to reception keen to shake him off whilst I got the key. I didn't, he hugged my back and rested his head on my shoulders, towards the desk which filled my heart with warmth but head with worry, then he said;

"Annie Harper," I cringed "*and guest*, checking in!" winking to me. *Cheesy!*

I blushed and clashed with the bright orange walls and wished the royal blue carpet lush with deep pile would swallow me up. "Actually its Turner, I requested room 104." I told the receptionist who was raising her eyebrows and looking bemused with my companion but handed me the key. I was being judged I realised. It was barely lunchtime and I was bringing a guy to a hotel who didn't even know my name! *I would judge me.*

"Its my work name," I said as we walked for the lift, "they paid for the room, I'm supposed to be working," I pushed my shoulder into him, "*remember*? I'll only throw my case in. If you want to stay down here, grab a cab, back in two." I entered the lift alone desperate to calm my skin down into a chilled colour before we entered daylight again.

I found my room, at the nice quiet end of the corridor. I had stayed here a few times before when I was *actually* working! It was OK. I threw my case towards the wardrobes. There was a sofa, desk, double bed and en-suite, all an 'over-nighter' needed in a rose chequered fabric. Checking my reflection on the mirror near the door - *OK* - I turned to open it…

*Smash! T*he door flew open missing my face by centimetres and I felt the rush of air whiz past me before…

Crack! Went my back onto the wall sending shards of pain up my spine…

Christ, I was being smothered, I could barely breath, I shook my head from side to side…

OH, I was being kissed!

Out of breath he pushed me back onto the wall, shoulders first this time and with a little less pain. *He must have took the stairs,* I thought whilst trying to get my lips to respond to his pouts.

I laughed, I didn't want to. This was passion, this was hunger but bigger than all that, this was relief. I grappled with his t-shirt after probably minutes. He had oh so smoothly hidden this desire from me far more than I him. He knew me well enough to know I wouldn't refuse him not that I did this often but he knew I had come here for this, for him. I had yearned for this and now it was happening. I slid my hands under his t-shirt as we frantically kissed. He was warm and smooth, not quite as smooth as he had been all those years previous. Now I could glide my fingers through chest hair and find two pert nipples.

We parted lips as our tops ripped over our heads. *Flesh.*

Our eyes met, this was it. I had wanted this to happen but never expected it to be so sudden. Huh, 'sudden' I smirked, I had known him over a decade.

He looked down at my breasts. Heaving in my new matching - *thank-goodness* - bra and cupped them. He ran his thumbs over my hard nipples, I gasped. His touch was sensational. He has me flustered at his near mere presence so his hand on me was exasperating. My bra was on the floor as my legs longed I was. They were quivering as the situation got deeper so did our inhibitions. I loosened his belt and jeans enough to see his underwear. I pushed my palm beneath the elastic top.

Bang bang bang

"Ms Turner? Security, is everything OK?"

WTF!

I stopped.

He didn't.

"Ms Turner, reception said a man ran to your room with hast and she was concerned."

He spread my legs, somehow I was naked! His cool tongue raced along my inner thigh, his fingers grappling along the outer.

"Ms Turner?"

I whimpered, partly in response to the banging door and partly as his touch had hit my insides.

Was he for real? I grabbed his hair, cracking the gel, puling him back then up, face to face. He pulled down his elastic I had fumbled,

"I'm fine, thanks!" Was all I could muster threw the door, politely anyway!

"But the The Man?" they continued to ask.

"...The Man is here, right here" he whispered as he slid me down onto him.

I bit my knuckle, "Yes, I know him, all's fine, thank you." I yelled to the inappropriate extra at the scene.

He pulled my legs off the floor and round his waist, right now the whole world could be banging on that hotel door. The conversation was over. He was plunging deep inside me.

The air was hot, quiet, full of breath.

The skin scuffed on my lower back on the cheap patterned wallpaper as we shuddered to a sweaty finish and I knew the scar left behind would be a reminder of today's ridiculous rushed but tasty events.

We kissed as we caught our breath, smiling in the pauses.

"Why?" he asked, "Haven't we done that before?"

How do you follow that? How had we crawled onto the bed afterwards and just lay, not sleeping, just being? Later I headed towards the en-suite. I needed a shower, so did he and so did the blanket I had left him wrapped in! I turned and just watched him as the water warmed. It had been the perfect way to get rid of the nerves. He lay head to the side. His dark hair fell over his left eye, no gel left to hold it in place! He was truly beautiful. It was true he could walk through a crowd and turn no heads. He could be quietly sitting at work and not muster any raised eyebrows but the moment he smiled women should melt. I didn't understand how he did it. We walked earlier through the crowds and women were walking past him and not looking twice. To me I would have stopped and drooled until he was out of sight. He wasn't plain, he wasn't 'boy band shiny' but he had 'It', whatever 'It' was. He was himself and he was exactly what my heart desired. I admitted, I loved this man. I held my stomach, it flipped, not with longing anymore but with guilt I shouldn't love this man.

I'm married!

That afternoon we wondered around the streets lined with groovy shops and smelling of donut stalls and sweet smelling candy floss making the day more carnival like than real life. The sun was still shining and so were we. We pottered about hand in hand pointing out weird things in shop windows that only visitors would buy, knitted union jack pot covers and double decker fag lighters. I'm sure all who saw us had no doubt we were together. I had no doubt we belonged together, we fitted together, we complemented, we knew each other, *now inside and out!*

Yet the feeling of his right hand in my left, the pressure of his fingers on mine, his skin on mine. His skin where my rings should be. The rings I'd pledged to where 'for better or worse', for life. I guessed the last few hours had been the 'for better' bit for me and the 'for wor*se*' bit for my husband, Andy.

Andy was a workaholic, its there at Time Publishing we had met 6 years earlier. It was a normal start, no fireworks. On a works night out I had drunkenly agreed to share a cab and apparently, as I found out the next night as he stood on my doorstep, I had also agreed to a 'dinner date'.

He was unusually healthy for a single man who lived alone. He had blonde spiky hair and was my height with the most usual green eyes. He looked after his appearance, was easily chatty, chivalrous (the first few months anyway) and a hard worker. All this equalled a very normal, safe guy and at that point in my life that's what I needed. We soon became 'Annie & Andy' - one thought, one person.

Andy worked hard in the week. Something that I had found attractive at first, ambition, structure, maturity. Now it worked against me. I was lucky if I got off on time at the office but at least as a Script Reader I could take my work home and reading them didn't seem so dull with a glass of red and a slab of diary milk in your own home!

Andy was the coordinator of whichever project Time had chosen to represent. It could vary from an autobiography, to short story film or fiction production. They all required Andy to place the people, the scripts, the time and distribute the pennies. Until close of launch or premier night Andy would be lucky to sleep in our marital bed 2 or 3 nights a week. Instead his work or home office choosing to send him to sleep at some ridiculous hour.

He loved his job and I loved mine. They were what we had both studied for and struggled from the bottom to earn.

In the days after the drama and before he next project we were happy together, though always doing 'something'. We could never just 'be'. He didn't set my world on fire. He didn't cause that stirring below my stomach when he kissed me, if he kissed me. It was more routine than want. Discussing gas bills and which broadband providers were cheapest wasn't exciting stuff. I'm not daft, I know passion and desire fade but a glimpse of it would keep me interested. It was a day-to-day relationship and everyone 'needed' normality right?

Back to today's reality and we chose a restaurant and sat down at a table. It was quiet for the capital but it was a strange time to be eating. We had missed lunch thanks to his pounding on a hotel wall, which had certainly worked up an appetite, and it was too early for dinner time trade.

We picked at our tapas, swapping memories which we never spoke of any other time except to each other. Memories that, without each other would just fade away. Occasionally I would try to feed him a prawn or two knowing full well he'd freak out, but he'd retaliate with offering an olive and a finger of couscous - *yuk!*

It was nice. Time passed we people watched and judged the oddities London had to offer. I wondered how many were here 'on-business' as I had lied, and how many were in love. Who were on first dates, last dates. How many marriage proposals had Leicester square seen? How many had lasted?

A bloody olive being poked at me jolted me back. I must have glazed over with my thoughts.

He looked at me, "So?" he asked, I'd obviously missed the question.

"So?" I repeated

"Are we going out later? You must have packed something in that monster suitcase suitable for a few drinks in town." *Oh yes, I thought, I've packed something though it's for our return. It would need Dutch Courage to be shown and as he had offered, a night on the town would do just fine!*

We got ready quickly considering the flesh on display. The sun peaked through the curtains and his skin glistened when he wondered about in his boxers that I'd pealed off earlier. His skin was slightly bronzed, thankfully not from this ludicrous fad that seems to be catching, sun beds, but from the actual real sun the late spring had offered. Though his luscious bottom remained white!

I hadn't attempted any more 'moves' as I had some hidden surprises under my dress for him later. Hopefully he was into this sort of thing. I wanted his eyes to pop. He had taken charge earlier and tonight it would be my turn. I rarely got to play out such scenes at home. It was hard to maintain pleasure when you were alone most nights, I wasn't about to dress up for a night alone. I had divulged in the mixed feelings of self satisfaction but a vibrator was only good for a quickie every so often, and wouldn't care what I was wearing!

Andy would more often than not come to bed tired and on the occasion we did sleep together it was more 'roll on roll off' once a month than the stuff I planned for later tonight.

With our first drinks I requested wine. It was a quicker accelerator to the boss I needed to be later but I had to slow down and ordered some long spirits as the night drew on. I wanted control not a drunken slapper shag!

We danced up the streets like the teenagers we once were not the early thirties we'd become. We jumped over benches, he swung me and balanced me on my now wobbly heels as I walked along the wall of the fountain during our walk home.

"Annie?" he was serious now. He stopped and pulled me towards him, for once I towered above as still standing on the wall. He hugged my legs, "What are you hiding?" *Shit! H*ad he seen the indent in my left finger, I had to think, I had no answers. "...under that dress?!" he finished, rubbing his fingers along the ridge of my suspender line, phew!

I ran and giggled all the way back to our hotel. Past a new receptionist and into the lift, together this time. I didn't let him catch me easily. He didn't muster much speed, intent on playing the game a little longer I thought. We reached the room and I kissed him hard whilst he fiddled to open the door.

My alcohol fuelled confidence led my hands

to follow his zip line and to my surprise his friend was already to play. No, I thought, not yet. I want those popping eyes first not gaping boxers.

I pushed him onto the bed. The curtains were closed but not the blackouts so there was flickers of light seeping through from the street lamps.

I rolled his t-shirt over his head and twisted it tight, with no hesitation he let me cover his eyes and took his hands under his head whilst I climbed over him and began to strip him.

First his socks and shoes. I kissed the bareness of his feet and stroked up around his ankles, he couldn't keep them still. My hands roamed up his trouser legs and I continued my kissing. Reaching up I undid his belt and lowered his jeans. My nails scrapped his inner thigh, he whimpered. Laying only with his underwear on I sneaked off the bed to undress myself.

I undid his blindfold and watched his eyes wonder over my scantily clad body. I wanted him to feel his way over the silk, run up my suspenders and over my barely there knickers. I placed his hands to my breasts to let him know he could. He sat up energetically kissing my neck. The kisses turned to snogs as tongues lashed against each other. His hands not knowing where to dart next. I let him wonder on top of my negligee but not under ensuring I still held the power.

He was hungry and harder to stop. I rammed his hands down to his side and sat him up against the headboard. His undergarments were coming off when his blindfold was re-applied.

I circled my tongue down his chest. Over his nipples towards his snail trail hair line, like a map blindly guiding me to a prize. His 'prize' well on its way I came up for air and let his fingers wonder into my expensive new knickers. I was so ready to let him explore and explore he did. His thumb brought me to the brink as I had him. I pulled his hands away before it was too late!

I mounted him. Sitting on top, both upright, both panting we began to rock slowly at first then harder. I wanted this to end together. I kissed him till we whimpered and he lifted his fine ass and me into the air as he stretched out in pleasure.

Exhausted we lay together not daring to move, to break the peace. Not wanting a new minute to happen and take our minds off the last euphoric moments.

He rolled to me, full in the face, eye-to-eye. I could feel his breath on my lips. I knew what was coming. I wanted to tell him too. To shout it from the rooftops but as he whispered those three little words softly whilst stroking my face it seemed the whole room was closing in.

"I'm married" I said. Guilt clutching my inners and retching with words in to his heart.

I rolled over to the edge of the bed, my back towards him. The once crisp white sheets now crumpled, empty between us. The silent tears drained and burned in my eyes. I do not know what he did, he remained still, silent.

The next morning I felt his hand on my shoulder rolling me before I opened my eyes from the conscious of sleep. I had fully expected a note of goodbye to appear on the opposite pillow to greet my eyes this morning. To my amazement he was still naked in bed, with me. Again he stroked my face. We smiled, did I still have him? Did he still want me? I put my hand to my head, he lifted it away and kissed my fingers, wrapping them through his. His eyes changed and he looked down. There it was, he'd remembered. He began to open his mouth but I didn't want regret, I had enough guilt of my own.

I kicked my legs over to the side of the bed to get out. My lingerie seemed silly now, ruffled with last nights mind blowing sex, inappropriate sex.

He pulled me back with a tug. Whatever he wanted to say I was obviously going to have to listen.

I searched his eyes but he wouldn't meet me, fiddling with my fingers which he still held in his hand.

"I'm married too!" he mumbled.

I laughed, I couldn't help it. Marriage vows obviously meant nothing in our friendship.

I kissed him. He turned away.

Who were we and what were we doing?

I had no idea what to say I wanted to say '*thank goodness*' but that felt heartless. His revelation had made me feel great and him awful. Now we shared something else - guilt. It wasn't eating me anymore, last night I had felt like the lowest person on earth. Cheating on Andy and falling for this beautiful upset man beside me.

I knew we were the same, I knew we were tied together but lived in another world. I knew as he finally began kissing me back that, yes I loved him, yes we belonged together, though in another life.

This time it wasn't frantic 'gotta have you now' sex like our first time or the dirty power struggle of last night; this time we made love. Slow, caressing and longing. Wanting to take in all of each other. We knew the truth, I was leaving in a few hours and returning to my marriage, back down the motorway and back to 'normal', and now I understood so was he. We were off limits and that's just the way to had to be.

It had taken me ages to get out of bed. Holding each other tightly. We didn't speak. I got up, dressed and threw everything else into my case.

He lazed in bed, not sleeping, not stirring at my noise. I was done packed to leave but not ready to go.

I climbed on to the bed, my hair fell over his face as he lay under me, the duvet parted us. I rubbed his nose with mine, as always and lightly kissed his fantastic lips, they really were my favourite part. They seemed softer and fuller than ever now I was leaving them behind. This is how I would remember him, surrounded in an igloo of my hair.

"See you Eskimo." I didn't look back, I grabbed my bag and opened the door. "I love you." I whispered to his memory as the door clicked closed.

TWO

The journey home was long. Yes a weight had been lifted and yes maybe this weekend could finally put our history behind us but thinking I had left those lips behind was not a happy thought. I guess we finally had closure. We had experienced life together in the form of a stolen weekend of absolute happiness but that was not the life we lived. It was fantasy and as I wiped the first rain of the weekend off my windscreen I looked forward, not back, for perhaps the first time in years.

I rang Andy when I was nearly home to help with my bags and the dinner I had picked up on the way home. He greeted me with the regular kiss on my cheekbone and took the bags on offer. I had picked up one of those takeaways you cook at home popping it in the oven for later I made some chat about my rubbish working weekend and headed for the shower.

Letting the water wash over me I let the last of him wash away. I hadn't showered since we went out for lunch the day of my arrival and up until the soap lather filled my nose I had smelled the hotel room sex from my every pore. This was going to be it. The shower tray emptied of his fragrance and I pulled on my welcomed dressing gown. I would not think of him again, I couldn't. I didn't regret my actions and my only guilt was towards him about Andy's existence but they were freed slightly when he chimed his wedding bells of truth too. I didn't have guilt for Andy. We had been living separately in one house for months. My attention had to be on saving my marriage and putting some of the energy from craving for my Eskimo into righting 'Annie & Andy's' wrongs.

A few months passed, Andy and I re-did our already beautiful house. It was the house of American tree lined soap opera roads but in suburban Sussex. Yellow brick and wooden porch it showed our wealth to the street as much as the next house. One good thing I still appreciated about Andy was his phenomenal salary. As his head was on the chopping block at Time if anything they put their name to flopped, he was paid a huge salary. Mine wasn't to shabby either.

We had a stunning home in a desirable village. We were able to afford to live by the coast and have fancy two-seater cars to drive into work in the city. I knew material possessions were worthless in the real world but if you had to be sad somewhere it was better being sad in good surroundings. We were the pinnacle of young professionals. The decorators were in and out as we made joint decisions. Visiting showrooms and choosing paints. The garden became my sanctuary and when Time called Andy back for the next instalment of a sequel.

I had surprised myself how quickly I had seemed to move on. That weekend my Eskimo and I seemed to have filled the 'What If' part of 'us' and now we knew, it seemed the need had gone. I thought about him yes, but differently now. I wondered about his house, his wife, his work. How his life was, the same as I would wonder about any old 'friend'.

I couldn't allow myself to think how long he had stayed in that bed that day. I couldn't wonder if he'd thought of me the journey home as I had him but mostly I couldn't allow myself the thought that, like me, he'd finally moved on too.

With an aching in my tummy I remembered I had yet to start dinner and actually missed lunch. I doubted Andy would be eating with me so I went back into the house for the evening, leaving my lovely thriving garden to fall under the cover of autumn darkness. I started to chop some peppers, onions and sealed them in a wok with my bean sprouts, adding the diced chicken and ladling in some earlier prepared thawed stock.

I took my 'make me feel better' soup into the snug and wrapped myself into a blanket. I stirred the golden hot liquid to absorb the salt and pepper I had added on my way past the counter. I leaned for the remote and felt a sharp stabbing pain in my abdomen. I breathed out loudly, moaning and it subsided. Lowering myself to sitting pains shot up my spine and I was in agony. I fell onto the sofa, doubling over, holding my tummy. This was way more than hunger and I needed the phone. Hurrying for breath between the stabbing pains and pushing my fist into my gut, it helped the pain, I managed to grab the phone.

"Something's wrong, I Need You!" I know I'm not good with pain at the best of times but I didn't want Andy to think it was like a 'paper cut' cry for help. I was in real pain. I was panting the words. My stomach was contracting and with it I felt faint.

To give Andy his credit he arrived home within 30 minutes, scooped me up and lifted me into his car. He did well not to panic as he wasn't normally so calm under pressure. I didn't know if an ambulance was needed, I didn't know what was happening. I just wanted someone else to take control. I let Andy be my guardian. I was pale and sounds were echoing as the scenery raced past the window. I was feeling the pain but this had to be happening to someone else. Things like this don't happen to me.

He continued to carry me as he burst through the emergency room doors. The pain increased when ever he moved and by the time Andy placed me on a bed in a side booth, I could barely breath. I couldn't lay flat and the crippling pain worsened with the doctors pokes and questions. Then the tops of my legs began to feel moist and I remember Andy's face when he saw the blood. He left the room as the doctor squeezed some warm gel onto my tummy and the mask someone was holding near me was making my head woozy.

"Mrs Turner, how far along are you?" I looked blankly, "The baby, your baby, there is still a heartbeat but we must determine which trimester you are in. Mrs Turner?"

Darkness filled my eyes from the outside in. Lightening shaped flashes sparkled from the lights. This feeling wasn't to do with the pain anymore or the odourless gas that someone was filling my nostrils with but the pending realisation - I was pregnant?

"A baby Annie, we are going to have a baby!" Andy was smiling broader than I had seen since our wedding photos when I awoke feeling groggy. The pain had gone but the confusion remained.

The scenery around me had changed. I was no longer surrounded by running doctors panicking questions to me. I was on a ward, a maternity ward. I was wrapped so tightly in a bed that had been made around me. I couldn't move my legs but I could feel them, naked against the hospital starched sheets. The robe I was wearing must be the kind open at the back and not long enough to cover my modesty. Normally all of these things would have sent my complaint gland into over drive but my head was fuzzy and Andy was harping on about telling people our news.

"The doctors think you're around 5 months, she's small but perfectly developing. She will probably be small all the pregnancy, you see Annie," he lowered his gaze and held my hand, "the bleed was another baby. We were having twins but only one foetus continued after the first trimester. They explained it all to me but its confusing. I'll get someone for you" he went to walk away.

"No!" I lifted my head "Did you..." I couldn't think, I felt awful. I needed water. "did you say she? She was developing?"

"Annie, we're having a girl!" he held out a sonogram picture of our new reality. Being pregnant was yet to sink in but hearing she was a girl, a daughter. This was too much. Andy's face as he pointed out her outstretched limbs, nose, umbilical cord etc, he lit up.

"...but we weren't going to have kids." I could see my honesty had shocked him, "You said it wasn't in our plan. We had careers not babies, we're DINKies," Double Income No Kids.

As Andy walked away I had to continue that train of thought. How are you supposed to change your life plan because of an accident? I knew at five months the decision was out of my hands. I was having this baby - this little girl. I was going to be a mummy and all my material possessions were going to sink into insignificance.

Telling people our news was a bittersweet. We'd start happily by introducing my slightly rounded belly as 'Bella' our soon to arrive daughter but we also had to tell them about 'Jacob', a son we'd never meet. We didn't want him never to have his moment, our son had died to save Bella, giving his space, nutrients and eventually his life to allow Bella to be in our lives. We had named him, mourned him, an idea of him anyway. We would tell Bella she was a twin and that he had gone to live on a cloud so she could always look up and feel him looking over her. He was her guardian angel. We weren't religious but the thought of him looking down on us reassured me everything that was unusually happening around here was happening for a reason.

Life had taken a dramatic overhaul. Not only was our future different it seemed to be with a different Andy too. He had become so considerate and charming, it made me feel like we should have taken the steps towards parenthood ages ago then maybe I could have looked back on happier memories with him than I actually had. Still the future was bright and I was happy again. Andy no longer worked late and being an 'office couple' he had found them fantastically supportive in our hour of need. Giving Andy all the time off he needed and instructing a minimum of two months recovery leave for me. The leave would pretty much take me up to the start of my 'surprise' maternity leave, give or take a few weeks cross over to train my stand in.

The midwife appointments were starting to get closer together as the weeks flew by. It was becoming increasingly difficult to aim into the sample pot they thrust at you in reception, instead warming my hands with this golden liquid everyone was suddenly so interested in! Each time I went I was told everything was fine and sent away. The appointments were only minutes long but the best part, hearing Bella's heartbeat, seemed to last for ages. It pumped away like a horses hooves hitting the ground racing at 110 beat per minute. Though the midwife had said everything was 'normal' it was only at that point that it seemed so.

It was a time I mourned again for my mother. Becoming a parent was such a surprise for me I had really needed someone with experience to guide me through. A mother, an aunt, a sister. I had none of these. The latter two had never existed but the first was cruelly taken away from me years before I was ready for her to go. My mother would never meet her grand daughter, she would never see her daughter become a mummy, her baby have a baby. It wasn't fair. It wasn't fair she was gone but it was especially unfair when I needed her so desperately.

Andy and I took the Christmas break to decorate the nursery. The firm always closed down the Christmas fortnight and with the winter sales we went silly and brought ridiculous amounts of stuff. We had gone for lemon in colour with antique white furniture. I had brought one of those posh rockers with a footstool to aid the midnight feeds. The mentality seemed to be 'if we're doing this, we're doing it in style!'. We had money to spend and who knows how long it would last after our bundle was here.

It turned out this was Andy's calling. He put all the furniture together with tools I never knew he had. He took me to baby shows and stalls galore. We had every gadget and gizmo, infact we had everything except a baby. With Bella due in the early spring, March, it gave us plenty of time to enjoy the preparation and maybe, relax a little.

Andy and I had got to know each other again and we spent many nights reminiscing. Honestly I had to be careful at this point. You imagine all the romantic memories in your head belong to you and your hubby but in actual fact I really had to scramble through the Ibiza and London ones and stolen weekends to find anything that we shared together!

At night he would prod my tummy to see if Bella wanted to play. Most nights I went to bed happy, with Andy's hand on my bump and my hand on his. She had brought us closer together, given us a vested interest. We were going to be a family and I would be forever grateful. She had saved me from my own thoughts, saved me from a 'normal' life and showed me that though my heart yearns it will never be so fulfilled as it will be by her.

We managed a quick weekend break away to Edinburgh in the new year. I was due back to work for one more week and Bella was pretty much ready soon after that so we wanted one last memory when we were just a twosome. It wasn't so much climbing the Scottish Highlands or wondering the streets for bargains. It was a pampered weekend mainly spent in a dressing gown. We lolled on sun loungers, indoors, lazed in the conservatory drinking hot chocolate and eating creamed scones. I got bigger and bigger and by the time I was ready for work the following Friday, my last Friday, I barely had anything other than jogging bottoms and Andy's t-shirts that fit me!

I took pride in being a normal size 12 and loosing the view of my feet didn't fit well with me. I missed my well earned clothes and had to make do with new handbags and shoes - after all no matter what size you may be they always remain a constant.

Our trip up to Scotland had been the last run for my beautiful two-seater sports car. It was a huge hurdle to get in and out of the thing at my size and it wasn't rocket science that it no longer suited our growing unit. Sadly they were not designed for baby seats and I think I would find myself a laughing stock at Asda cramming a baby and a weekly shop in the boot!

It was a sad day I handed over the keys, like I was handing over the keys to my youth. I know at nearly 31 'youth' had probably all but disappeared but driving it made me feel successful, cool even.

The day I part ex'ed my car for my 4x4 was the day I grew up, became a women. No longer a young lady confused with what she wanted. It was the day I became a mummy - well a pending mummy anyway!

With Andy's two-seater still parked on the drive it would not be a constant remainder what I had given up but what I had to look forward too, and besides my 4 x 4 could squash Andy's Z3 whenever I pleased!

As I drove in to work for the final time I noticed how wintry everything still was. The frost on the evergreens outside our house stood out, like I could start to enjoy my surroundings and not just rush past them in a frenzy to work. It was the last day in February and still deep winter, the frost made me walk like a penguin over the car park. Under normal circumstances you walk cautiously but imagine carrying an 8 month old pregnancy bump over ice, on heels, not clever Annie.

Andy was sticking to early morning arrivals at the office so I arrived alone. They had yet to find me a replacement so my workload was simply to put my job down in procedures so a replacement could pick up where I left off. It suited me fine. I slurped my coffee. My entrance had mainly consisted of present collection from well wishers and hearing again many births stories from every women who had ever had a baby or anyone they knew had. It was hard to hear birthing stories, I had heard many and people certainly didn't think they should tone them down simply because I was going to experience it sometime soon. Invariably there was always some kind of drama and lots of blood.

My last job was to empty and forward my email inbox, I'd left it till last as I am a hoarder and keep everything. Mostly I hit the delete button but then staring up from the monitor was something to make my eyes pop and my heart race.

INBOX (1)
SUBJECT: ESKIMO CALLING?

In my fragile state I could barely breath. I felt like all eyes were on me, suddenly I was burning up and convinced myself all was aware, like there was a neon sign above my head saying 'inappropriate behaviour about to occur'. I pulled the chair as close to the desk as Bella would let me get, took a deep breath and double clicked enter to open it.

I NEED TO SEE HIM, THE MAN YOU MARRIED. I CANT SHAKE IT. I NEED TO SEE THE MAN WHO KEEPS YOU FROM BEING MINE. X

My eyes were darting about. The email had been sent today, about 20 minutes ago. I pictured him sat at his PC, waiting for a reply. He had used our shared email account, eskimocalling@hotmail.com to contact me. I had forgotten I always had that route to get to him. We had set it up years ago when one of us changed our mobile number without realising and I had received a strangers response to my 'eskimo calling?' text that I imagine would melt an igloo!

The thoughts I allowed myself to think hit me like a train. 'WHO STOPS ME FROM BEING HIS'? I had been so focused not to think of him and now I had Bella to put all my thoughts into. This was the first time I had pictured him. I wondered how his hair had grown, what he was wearing. It was early still, was he at home or at work? I had daydreamed long enough, time to answer. I searched our online photo vault and chose a wedding picture and a recent one.

YOURS TOO X. I replied, attaching the pics.

I had long imagined what his wife looked like. What kind of women had bagged him, perhaps from me?

I waited anxiously, not for long, his reply was pretty instant.

ANNIE, YOU'RE PREGNANT?

I hadn't noticed I had sent a pregnant one. It was a picture from our Edinburgh trip recently and I just saw that Andy looked good so sent it.

Ping, another message:

ANNIE, IS IT MINE?

The realisation hit me with a hard punch. 'Yes' my mind instantly said.

Why had this happened today? Today my last day here. I could have gone on convincing myself everything was fine and I was happy, Bella was coming and Andy would be a good dad if the 'pregnancy Andy' was anything to go by. If he sent it tomorrow it would have been returned to sender, no address known. Is that what I really wanted?

A huge question mark hung over my head and the family life I had planned hung in the balance. Messages filled my inbox, SUBJECT: ESKIMO CALLING?, but struggling to breath I grabbed my bag and ran to the loo.

I pulled out my diary when safely in a booth, flickering through the pages of dates and working backwards from our meet in June. The moment the thought of paternity hit me I knew Bella wasn't Andy's, maybe subconsciously I had always known. I knew now no matter how hard I tried I couldn't ever forget him. In a few weeks time I'd be holding his baby, I'd be forever tied through this gorgeous bump, that weekend and my beautiful lover.

The tears burned my eyes and wet my face.

Then my waters broke and wet my legs.

THREE

I frantically called for Jenny, our receptionist, she had seen me fly in here and was the closest pair of ears to the toilets.

I knew Andy would freak out and run us to the hospital for Bella to join us but I couldn't think about that now. Yes I was in labour weeks early and yes I had had a very scary pregnancy but right now I had to get to my PC, I had to delete his emails.

"Annie, is that you? Everything OK?" asked Jenny "Oh Jesus!" she exclaimed as her inappropriate four inch 'work' heals slapped down on the wet floor.

I managed to stand and opened the door, "Jenny?" she'd gone, with one guess where.

Andy hit the door running, followed by Jenny and a chair covered in a shopping bag, no doubt housing someone's lunch until my drama revealed itself!

"I'm fine, we've got plenty of time yet," I staggered forwards not in pain but trying to stop the dripping clothes clinging to my legs. "I'll finish what I was doing and we'll say some goodbyes and then leave eh?" I started for my desk casually, hopefully.

Andy looked scared. "Annie we are leave Now!"

Something in his statement made me look to the floor, he wasn't just scared, that was a command.

The toilet floor was wet, wetter than I had thought, yes my waters had gone and with the pressure building in my abdomen there was no doubt labour was coming but the floor wasn't clear water, it was red. Blood red.

As the situation set in I panicked. I launched for Andy and he carried me in the direction of the sirens that were coming round the bend and pulling up outside.

The tears for my email predicament were taken away by sobs of worry. Trying to hold them in and not tell of my turmoil was like trying to hold back a sneeze.

The ambulance rocked with speed. I should have been freezing laying there in my work clothes no time to grab a coat but I was warmed by fear. Fear for too many things for my mind to concentrate on and keep to myself all at the same time. I lay with my hands on my bump, holding on to her, wanting a reassuring kick that never came. Andy held his head in his hands. I had never wanted children but the thought of never meeting this bundle I had created scared me rigid. I reached for Andy's hands. We needed to be together now, strong, for our daughter.

But no, she wasn't his daughter was she. I groaned. I had managed to tell Jenny to turn my PC off as we left. I told her I only had junk emails and that my work was complete so my account could be suspended. I had even remembered earlier to put my 'out of office' reply on to start tonight. That problem was sorted. My secret only had two blips. Emails one, and the real baby daddy was the other. He would never believe I would keep him from his own child. If he doesn't hear from me he'll assume he was wrong. Continue as he had last week when he'd forgotten about me and lived his life with his wife, maybe even his own kids.

Was I really going to keep this up, for life? Lying to Andy and Bella. Andy had changed at her prospect. We were happy again, looking forward and sharing our new life. Looking at the worry in Andy's eyes now. He kissed our joined hands. He was whispering prayers, whispering to anyone who would listen. Asking for everything to be OK. We knew Bella would be small, not only because she was early but because she had struggled from the beginning. She had battled everything thrown at her so far in her very short existence. She could win one more, that I was sure of.

We were rushed straight to theatre. I knew a c-section was likely. I didn't think they could risk Bella the trauma of labour and birth. They erected a screen over my bump. Andy joined me dressed in scrubs and a mask. The lights were bright against my eyes and I was faced up towards them when everyone one else was looking down. I had been put in another of the gowns that disagreed with every part of me and with a large bump popping out the front it barely covered around my sides let alone my back. There was no smell to the room. I thought it should smell clean, of TCP or antibacterial solutions but it didn't. I hoped I wasn't going to be one of those Panorama stories from dirty hospitals or having swabs left in me!

They told me from the lower end of the screen that the procedure only takes minutes, its the sewing up that takes the time. I didn't care. I wanted her out. I could hold her whilst they did what they needed with me.

I felt a tugging. I had read it might feel like someone was doing washing up inside me!

Then I was empty.

She didn't cry. Bodies filled the room surrounding my baby. Bleeps from machines being turned on waved on the silent air. Andy had gone over to see her, leaving me.

He returned, in his arms lay my baby, my tiny baby. Andy was smiling, was all well?

He lay her on my chest. I took in her smell, indescribable. I stroked her small head and she cried. At last she had made her existence know. Everything was OK. She had to go to the neonatal unit to be assessed for her first 24hrs because of her gestation. I didn't mind, all was well and at last I could sleep knowing she was here.

As I handed her back to Andy she opened her

eyes, Andy lowered her blanket under her chin and I saw her full face for the first time.

My stomach lurched. Even if I hadn't have received that email today or worked out some dates, at that moment I would have known. Those big plump lips, so red on her new skin. Those eyes, dark and deep. There was no denying her heritage.

With her blankets wrapped round her they took her away and I whispered, "Goodbye mummy's little Eskimo".

When I woke up, I was on the ward and it was dark. All the other mums had their babies by their beds. Asleep in their cots, doting mums leaning over them, checking they were breathing every 5 minutes and smiling at their achievement.

I turned. Next to my bed lay no cot, just a picture the nurses had taken for me to long at. I picked it up. Her eyes glared at me. Though a girl she oozed her fathers looks. She had a wisp of my white blonde hair and thankfully her weight was good for her gestation.

Eventually one of the new mums asked me about the whereabouts of my baby with a concerned, 'You OK?'. She wondered over, careful to leave her own baby in its crib so as not to show him off in front of me, 'just in case'.

When I told her, the whole room started to talk to me. Now I wasn't an emotional minefield of baby death or disorder. The cubicle held four ladies. All willing to tell and re-tell their story to anyone who'd listen. Maybe that's your prerogative, once you have experienced that much pain, too share it around. Huh, I suddenly understood all those birthing stories I was made to hear!

By the time the daddies began to arrive and my new 'friends through pain' returned to their beds leaving me alone again, I found myself thinking back to Bella's conception. Our weekend seemed so long ago, like a different lifetime. Yet it had created my present, my baby, my Annabel - 'Bella'. I could go along with this. I could raise my daughter with Andy. Telling the truth would only hurt people. It would ruin lives, mine and Andy's marriage couldn't stand adultery, we had always said so. Who knows what life would be like. I had to give Bella the best start after what she had been through. I had concluded: Andy would be the daddy. He would make a fantastic one. I could hold this secret. I could calm my cravings for my lover through looking into Bella's eyes everyday and remind myself of our lost lifetime.

At two weeks old we were finally aloud home. It wasn't even her due date yet but we were bringing her through our front door and home.

Our discharge came just at the right time, before my sanity disappeared completely. I had had enough of seeing 'newbies' come and go in 24 hours and some were being offered a 'fast pass', like we were at an Alton Towers attraction - six hours and they were out of here! Infuriating to say the least. Daily life was gruelling and things that you took for granted at home were a chore in hospital. Getting a cup of tea meant waddling down the corridor like John Wayne. All the other new mums looking on knowingly yet the dad's and visitors looking at you in pity. Screwing their faces at your pain then whispering behind an erected hand to their counterparts. There to was also 'the baby who didn't sleep'. It was never Bella.

It was weird too because no-one helped you. That might sound selfish but you'd think with a ward of nurses someone would offer help to the young 17 year old baffled by her new born or the mother who hadn't slept all night because of the above mentioned. Or help me when I wondered how I shower without leaving Bella by herself. But alas it seemed I did leave Bella by herself whilst I frantically try and waddle to the facilities, somehow remain standing whilst bending enough not to rip my surgery scar or bang my head on the shower fitting! All this to get back onto my ward to hear a baby crying and pray it wasn't my own.

I wanted to slob on my own sofa, wear my dressing gown all day if I chose and not have some nursing assistant suggest I take a bath and get dressed as soon as they turn on the lights at 6:30am.

I longed for home.

Andy had organised some friends and family to be at the house as a welcoming. To be honest I wanted peace and quiet but his goodwill was thoughtful.

We lay Bella down in the centre of the room in her moses basket. She slept whilst all cooed over her every twitch. 'Ooo'ing and Ahh'ing' every time she moved like she was a little pink firework! It was so nice to be home. The familiar faces were nicely looking after me and though the questions over labour/ birth and her dramatic entrance tired me I continued to answer them.

It saddened me that nobody mentioned Jacob, not even Andy had since we lost him that scary afternoon when our lives changed. I had looked sadly at only one crib in our lounge and all the pink surroundings. I wondered if Jacob too would have had his fathers beauty. Watching him grow into the essence of his father and seeing him bewilder young girls as he realised he was something special.

Every time Bella had kicked me I thought about how much more I would have been kicked if there were two in there. Whenever we brought anything I thought about the double expense we would have incurred buying it in blue too. As Bella grows up I'm sure I will wish she had someone to share it all with. Always having a playmate, a best friend to witness every part of life at exactly the same age.

I knew forming future memories of my son that never was, was unhealthy but it's something I couldn't help. Eventually I would get over never meeting him but having Bella just arrive home was an emotional time that brought it all to the surface.

It was Jenny who brought me out of my daze. Strange that she was here I thought - the only work person invited. Still I realised she called the ambulance and helped on Bella's arrival day so maybe she was curious to see and meet this child who had caused such a commotion.

"Long afternoon?" she questioned.

I smiled, "Repetitive!"

"She's a beauty Annie. She's made Andy a new man. She's all he talks about at the office whilst you've been in hospital with her," *I didn't know he'd been in the office*, I thought. She continued, "It seems trivial now but I turned your PC off as you asked." *Phew* "You did have some unread mail, all from the same address. I didn't know if it was junk or not, didn't want to delete the wrong thing so I just printed all that days emails off," I sat open mouthed, what the hell did this mean? Was she here to ruin our arrival home? Had she read them? Oh Christ what had she done with them?

"Its probably the last thing on your mind but I've popped them in an envelop and left them on the side in the kitchen. I think they're just junk, all of them marketing rubbish for some *'eskimo something'*. I didn't read them." She was lying.

It was hot in here now. There was no way I could hobble into the kitchen unnoticed. People had been offering me help with everything under the sun all afternoon, but I Had to try. I excused myself from Jenny and headed in the direction of the kitchen. I didn't meet anyone's eye and tried to keep my pace to non-panic stroll . I had gotten within a few steps, I could see the manila envelop on the counter when I felt burning in the back of my head and turned to see Jenny following my move. W*as she smirking?* I finally had my hands on the envelop when Andy engulfed me into a big hug from behind. He was so happy. I had felt his pride all afternoon, introducing '*his*' daughter to the visitors all day.

"People are leaving, will you come and say goodbye?" he turned me in the direction of the waiting smiley faces of the well wishers and away from the envelop.

A lot of hugs and kisses later we were finally alone with 'our' girl. I had managed to hide the envelop as Andy waved off the stragglers. I hadn't read the contents but at least it was out of eye sight. I would get a chance to read them later when Andy put my little Eskimo to bed and went up for a workout and subsequent shower.

I pottered about for a bit and even grabbed ten minutes shut eye on the sofa as Andy tided the pots from earlier. It gave me a chance to think if I wanted to read my lovers mail hiding in that envelop. I was sure he wouldn't be angry, it was not his style, unlike Andy. He would be questioning me out of concern. Would he be wanting me, wanting us to be a family? I couldn't be sure. Did I want that? I didn't know. Yes it would be nice to be wanted but the hearts that would break and the wounds it would cause. I had made the decision to cut him out before and I would stick to it. I had to didn't I?

It was early evening when Andy said he would take Bella upstairs to bed on his way to our gym as I had hoped. I had just finished feeding her and her eyes rolled with sleep as he took her off me.

I waited for her mobile to sound above her cot and the familiar whirling of Andy's machines starting up before I dare open the envelop now burning in my hands. I knew I had until I heard the shower before Andy would be down, perhaps an hour.

There were about ten pages all together, none more than a few lines. His thoughts popping into his head and send.

The first was the one I had replied to about a photo of Andy. The second, the statement that had sent me running to the ladies with my diary. The third was simply, ANNIE...?

By the fourth and fifth his words and thoughts were concerned.

Fourth: WHATEVER YOUR REPLY I'LL RESPECT IT.
Fifth: I KNOW YOU ANNIE. I KNOW THIS FEELING I AM GETTING.
Sixth: THIS WILL EAT AT YOU.

Seventh: THIS WILL EAT AT ME.
Eighth: I KNOW YOU WOULDN'T HIDE IT FROM ME WITHOUT REASON.

The ninth was longer, a few hours had past from the last. His address lay tiny in italics at the bottom of the pages, 'just in case' I guessed.

DEAREST ANNIE
I CANNOT STOP THINKING ABOUT THIS. I THINK I KNOW THE ANSWER I THINK YOU ARE GROWING OUR CHILD IN YOUR BEAUTIFUL BODY. I KNEW WHAT HAPPENED IN LONDON WAS SPECIAL. WE'VE ALWAYS HAD A CONNECTION. FROM OUR FIRST MEETING WE'VE BEEN PULLED BACK TOGETHER EVERY COUPLE OF YEARS NOW WE HAVE A BOND. A BOND THAT IS BIGGER THAN ANY REASON NOT TO BE TOGETHER.
ANNIE I LOVE YOU WITH EVERY BONE IN MY BODY.
SOMETHING MADE ME CONTACT YOU AGAIN ANNIE.
BE MINE? X

The tenth was from another few hours later. It read like he'd taken my silence as rejection. It was over. It simply read:

THIS WOULD HAVE BEEN AMAZING. GOODBYE ANNIE. X

Like a bolt of lightening I sat up. He was right. Like a slap in the face. Yes, it would be amazing. We were meant to be together, I could see that now. Sometimes your own feelings matter more. You only have one life and you should live it with someone who makes you feel how he makes me feel. The love we share would grow and heal the carnage the truth would cause. Andy would hate me anyway for cheating, he wouldn't want to raise another mans child. I would leave him everything except her, My daughter and I would do it tonight.

Excitement began to grab my tummy. Imagining life with him. I imagined his face as I arrived on his doorstep with her. Who would he hold first? I was what he craved but now I had to share him. I wouldn't be jealous of my own daughter. Infact sharing her simply made me want him more.

I raced up the stairs. I would need to pack a bag. Thankfully, though Bella needed a lot of stuff, it was mostly still packed from our hospital stay. She was stirring, perhaps she could feel the same vibrations that were now coursing through my body. I poked my head through her door and couldn't help but go in for a cuddle. We were about to go on an adventure together. An adventure that would shape our lives, our future.

I kissed the top of her sweet smelling head, "Let me tell you about your *real* daddy," I whispered.

"THAT WOULD BE GOOD!" the door flung open and Andy stood there. He was red, red with anger not red, hot with sweat.

I clung to Bella.

His arms were flying everywhere as he screamed at me. In his hands were papers flapping along with his arms.

"Andy?" I questioned, "Shh, you'll scare Bella."

He came towards me screaming. I picked up words like 'London' and 'working away'. He was furious pushing objects over and pacing.

"What's going on?" I nervously asked,

"What's going on?" he mocked. "What's going on you slut is that you've been caught out. You and your dirty secret. Passing your guilt onto me by posing that thing," he gestured towards Bella, "was mine. She's not mine, she's his. Get out of my sight, GET OUT!"

He pushed over a chest of drawers and got closer, "Andy you are scaring me and Bella's..."

"I don't care what I'm doing to that...that bastard baby of Yours."

I jumped past him and out to the landing, Bella had been given the biggest of the spare bedrooms but right then it felt tiny with him shouting on top of me.

"Don't forget these" he flung the papers at me,

they fell to the floor. My emails. I grappled to catch one. They were duplicates of what I had been reading downstairs.

"Fucking Jenny!" I mustered.

"Trying to hold on to every piece of him are you?" he came towards me again, raging.

I wanted to plead my apologies but I had to run. He was mad and nothing was going to come of this tonight. I grabbed Bella's heavy bag. I could cope with having nothing until he had calmed down and I could return alone for some belongings.

Juggling a bag, rushing away and holding Bella I made the stairs.

"Don't forget this," he yelled and threw me a 'daddy loves me' t-shirt someone had brought to the home welcoming earlier.

It was all it took for me to lose my balance. I fell backwards, releasing the bag and holding Bella closer. I hit the banister with my back and fell forwards nutting the step edge. Down to the bottom step and onto our tiled floor.

My head smashed on the cool floor and my eyes followed as Bella's body fell free from me. She fell three foot from my reach. As my eyes glazed over I could feel the blood running over my forehead like the touch of my mum wiping the pain away when I was young only the pain was increasing. Everything went hazy and my last vision was the slow trickle of blood coming from my little Eskimo's ear.

I lost Bella on the way to the hospital. Severe head trauma combined with her age had meant she had fought and lost her last fight. I didn't feel anything, I couldn't, I myself was in Intensive Care in a coma that would take me 5 weeks to come out of. The news of my baby's death would be the first thing I read on a piece of paper by my bed. Andy's handwriting spilled my heartache. He left his wedding band on the top, keeping the hurt still until I could move to read it.

FOUR

Our affair hadn't taken long to develop. What with me always working late and her being the office receptionist. I guess it was a cliché but right now it felt like a damn good one.

Jenny would always know when the office was empty. She'd see them leave at various minutes past clocking off, then she'd slink in to my office. The opaque glass doors did nothing to hide her approach. I could feel her coming and a whisper of a figure would appear. As the silhouette got larger so did my excitement. Jenny had turned out to be one hell of a women. Some things she knew and willed onto me had shocked, a women of her age, though 50 isn't old but for partaking in the things she did, it was far from young.

It was a far cry from my sex life with my wife. Annie was more of a home-bird. Intent on having a pleasing home and not pleasing a husband. Yes she was strong willed and yes we did sleep together, though rarely. Neither made the effort anymore and when routine implied we had gone too long a quick motion was all it took.

Sometimes I would sleep at the office after my fling with Jenny, partly due to not wanting Annie to see me creased and guilty and partly because I was knackered. The women was insatiable. There was a time when to escape them both I could go to my home office. Annie believed I was busy enough to say at the company office to work so staying in my study at home needed no excuse. The expensive leather chair and deep mahogany desk made the perfect Mans Cave feel and left me happy with the world. But Jenny was another matter. Seeing excuses as a challenge. She didn't take it lightly when I suggested I actually did have to work and gave me an IP address and web cam. Here she indulged in another of her fantasies - virtual sex.

Five minutes ago Jenny had entered my office. I could see the hunger in her eyes. This women used orgasms like coffee. She had sashayed across the office, making hardly a dent in the luxurious piled carpet like she was floating, slid between me and my glass desk and clicked down the receiver ending my call.
Silently, except for her evil grin she unzipped my fly and aroused me with her touch.
Four minutes she'd been scrapping my inner thigh with her nails and engorging her mouth up and down my shaft, taking care never to hit my tip, she knew then it would be over in seconds.
Its ridiculous how for the last three minutes I've

been replaying this in my head so I finally gripped the arms of my chair, leaned back and enjoyed her professional job.

I got in around 9:30pm, late enough to not have to do the 'evening' routine - cook, eat dinner, TV, tea, bed - with my wife but early enough to still be sharing a bed that night so I wouldn't get another nagging the following day.

As we unusually tucked up under the duvet together Annie leaned to me.

"I'll be away at the weekend, Time have managed to get that interview but I've got to go to her and she's in London. I should only be gone 1 night. I made some dinners and froze them so you wont go hungry."

"OK." I managed, did I care? *Honestly?*

Don't get me wrong I love my wife. She's great to have around for dinner party's, get-togethers and party's. We are both career people so thankfully no boring kids stuff to batter away. But she didn't set my world alight. Like I think Ludicrous says on the Usher track 'Yeah' - "We want a lady in the street but a freak in the bed!". Not that I consider myself to have much in common with a young black rapper but he was right. My wife was my 'lady' and Jenny was the 'freak in my bed'.

There was a time a felt enlightened when Annie entered the room. She was beautiful when we first got together and it wasn't her lose of looks that made me 'play away', infact if anything she was probably prettier. It was the routine, pattern and boredom, marriage itself perhaps had killed the excitement for me. I had her and she had me. Effort was no longer needed.

The idea had hit me whilst I probed Jenny against my overflowing desk the next evening. Again she had disrupted my work schedule, which as it happened not only was it full, hectic, but was now crumpled under her naked cheeks.

She'd got the seduction of me down to a tee. In she had wondered lifting her skirt to reveal lacy stocking tops. Facing the door and her back to me, she lay back onto my desk and pulled me towards her, upside down. She pulled on my tie and I followed her gaze as she pulled me round my desk. I was already hard at the sight of her readiness for me but as she rode her legs up straight besides her, split like, on my desk and I caught sight of her. My trousers throbbed at the view I saw, no knickers and just her, already moist waiting for me.

She grappled at my paperwork as I plunged deeply into her. It was rare she came before me but she quivered and I knew she had used me in her hour of erotic thought for complete selfish pleasure.

I stood up my wedding photo Jenny had knocked over during our encounter, I panged with guilt at the sight of our happy smiling faces.

"Annie's away this weekend." I grinned "We

could have a more comfortable setting next time?" I meant a hotel, this office lark was getting painful and there was nowhere to rest!

"Umm marital beds are for marriages not lovers." she quipped "But I'd like to see where you see me on my web cam."

Shit! Was I prepared to have my wife and lover overlap in one location. *Think fast Andy,* but she was gone pulling down her skirt just before opening my door.

Annie left early in the morning for the capital. I worked out in our home gym a little figuring a should get a good work out with in Jenny later! I waited a little after lunch to text Jenny my address. I had wanted to make sure Annie had gone and to remove some wedding pics and happy photos from my desk, their eyes would only hinder my later performance. How bad could having her here be? This was my domain, she was not in control here. We would see my study if she so desired then onto somewhere out of town, discreet. I wanted to see if this affair could move on from frantic sexathons.

The bell rang and I answered expectantly. Strangely there was just a box laying on our front porch with a note. I opened it. I never was one to open cards before presents. In the lining lay a pair of hand cuffs, the note read:

TILL TOMORROW. J x.

I had been let down? I guess this meant I was still a pawn in her game, whether here or at the office.

The rest of the day I managed to get the work done I never can when Jenny is around and the evening plodded by with tea and Annie's frozen meals. I actually smiled whilst tucking in. She did look after me. She was a good looking lady, certainly a catch. Though I worked out for my slender figure Annie had always been a lovely size 12. Not stupidly thin as the fashion seemed to enforce nowadays. Young girls ridiculously giving up carbs and eating nothing but low calorie milkshakes or some vile green slop that's supposed to be good for you but does nothing other than give you bad breath! Thankfully Annie liked hot buttered toast too much to waste her time and energy on counting points or giving up the good tastes in life. Her confidence is what shone as bright as her vivid blonde natural hair. She was my kind of height which looked good in photos. She was the kind of girl you always like but never approach for fear of being laughed away. The kind of women you didn't need to waste breath on asking if you liked her or not - it was a given.

From our first date I couldn't believe she had chosen me, and especially when I asked her to marry me. I remember thinking we'd be that couple at the party where all the guests look at us and wonder why She was with Me. They'd assume

I had money or was fantastic in bed, neither of which I minded! Having bagged her early with no hardship the challenge had gone and so had the pride in bagging her. What I had learnt from all this heat with Jenny was I was probably more of a love maker than a player. Dipping my toe, or any other part of my anatomy Jenny pleased, into the office pool wasn't thoughtful and actually normality didn't suck. Me and Annie had love. There is a great statement in the film The Mexican - two people have love but cannot make it work, how long until they call it quits?! The answer is Never, love is what you need to make the rest work. It was like the statement was just reaching me. I loved this women. Maybe it was the beer I had consumed but as I looked at her photo in my hand I realised just how stupid I had been. Risking it all, risking her for a quick leg over. Right then and there I called it off in my mind with Jenny - *was I stupid*? It was time I stuck to my vows and showed my wife I cared for her. I picked up the phone to call her. It was late now but she wouldn't mind, everyone likes to be told they are loved, right? Her voicemail clicked in and I clicked off. I didn't want to assemble the right and wrongs of our marriage on voicemail. I placed my mobile on the arm of the sofa, clumsily sitting on the remote which found some random Eskimo documentary on the Discovery Channel.

I had no idea when Annie would be home or

when Jenny would show. I was nervous, could today be the day I finally mess up my marriage hours after realising I want it saved?

Last night I had gone to bed full of confidence Annie was my future. I had wasted effort on Jenny and now I was going to put it all into righting it again. I wanted to become 'Annie and Andy' once more.

I jumped when the bell rang again, stupidly because Annie would have used her key!

Jenny sauntered into our hallway. Just seeing her here, in my home was wrong. Way wrong. She had that expectant look in her eyes. To be fair she had come here today for a sure thing and had no idea of my 360 degree change of heart since her package arrived. I needed to end this before she penetrated my marriage and home anymore.

"Jenny I.." she threw herself at my lips, we didn't normally kiss, but I managed to grab her by the shoulders. Jenny wasn't a women to mess about. She liked the direct approach so I came out with it. "Its over, I'm going back to my wife!" She sunk under my grasp. The floor length coat lifted off her shoulders as they dipped in disappointment revealing, well, nothing much! I thought she was upset until I felt her unbuckle my belt.

"If this is about me bailing yesterday," she continued, her hands now unbuttoning my jeans, "it was to make you wait, want me more. Is that the reason?"

"Well yes and no." I said "Not having you here made me realise I didn't miss you. All this heat was great for a while but what have we got other than sex? I miss my wife, I miss normality, I miss having a relationship. I miss Annie. I chose her." I grabbed her hands stopping her motion. I was sure I wanted this to end but if she made it inside my briefs I wasn't sure I could be so strong. "I chose Annie." I repeated.

What a mistake that was. Her arms flew over her head. Without all the screaming noises she was making she looked like she might take off!

Scarily she had left the hallway as I redid my jeans. She was heading towards the kitchen. She slid up onto the breakfast bar. Undoing the coat buttons to reveal another strange piece of lingerie that to be honest scared me more than turned me on. Some looked like pieces of torture and I never really got the hang or point of any of it. It just ended up on the floor, getting me flustered by battling to take it off not at the sight of it.

"Come on!" she jeered "Screw me!"

For once I was repulsed by her 'offering it on a plate' attitude. She looked wrong, she was infecting my home with her sexual prowess and I just had to get her out.

The phone rang and I turned to answer. It was Annie. She was five minutes away and would need help with her bags. I could thank god for the heads up later but right now I had to get this house emptied of my past.

I turned round to push Jenny, if I had to, out the door but she had gone. I didn't feel happy, I felt the opposite infact. I knew it wasn't going to be that easy. I knew she hadn't left of her own accord so where the hell was she? *Oh,* I turned my head and followed her thrown pieces of clothes up the stairs and into my and Annie's bedroom. *Shit!* I threw her clothes at her.

"Get Up and Get Out!" I shouted. I have a terrible temper when I am angry. It has caused me many problems in my younger drinking jealous days. Jenny's eyes lit. Of course, this sick women was going to get off on my anger.

Beep beep

Annie pulled into the driveway. Jenny locked her fingers together on her naked chest, they didn't move, they never did! "Now this is interesting!" she smirked.

"Stay there." I changed my tone to hushed, "Get dressed."

I ran down the stairs and out the back.

Annie didn't greet me, just thrust bags in my direction. Her actions panged me. I kissed her on the cheekbone as was usual now. This is what I wanted to change I thought. This is the lady I wanted to lust after again and have her want me right back.

I put the bags in the hall. I knew Annie would want them upstairs but I also noted she'd brought a 'cook at home take-away' so her putting it in the oven and faffing with the bags would give me enough time to get Jenny out, *hopefully*.

I raced up the stairs, taking two at a time. Right now my marriage depended on getting this nympho out of my home unnoticed. To my surprise she was dressed and standing at the window with, *god,* my wedding photo in her hand.

"I want you." she said "I want you like this. What you've got here - the love in your eyes. I want you to look at me like you do her. I want a relationship." She started for the stairs and out. "I'll leave now," she blew me a kiss "so you can leave Annie, I'll give you a few days." And she was gone. Someone really was on my side today.

"Psycho!" I whispered as Annie entered the room. *That was cutting it fine Andy.*

"Waste of time going." she moaned. "Rubbish weekend, rubbish work. I'm heading for the shower." and she too was gone. Leaving me in a room that minutes early held my fate in its balance.

Annie came down the stairs a changed women that day. Maybe I was giving off a different aura, approachable because she came to sit with me on the sofa and hunched herself under my arm.

A FEW MONTHS LATER

Finally it seemed I had the life and partner I wanted. As a new start Annie suggested we redid the house and she started the garden as I returned to being busy at work.

Jenny had gotten bored of waiting and the idea of a relationship thankfully, and had moved on to more unsuspecting pray. Someone younger and new to the office. It made me sad when I saw her disappear into the stationary cupboard with him panting after her. Not sad because it wasn't me but sad to think she was at it again. It seemed so irresponsible now, and so bloody obvious. Surely everyone knew what was happening. I cringed at the thought of my stupidity. Jenny had shown me a brief want of normality behind all the brass the day she showed up at my house and now it seemed she'd continue with her antics until she was bored again.

I was busy putting together the new trailer when my mobile rang with Annie's number.

"Something's wrong, I Need You." she said.

It would take me at least three quarters of an hour to get home at this time of day. We live in the country but worked in town. Somehow Annie's panicked statement made me reach her in just half the time.

When I reached home she was pale, laying on the sofa. There was spilt soup on the plush cushions, expensive rug and carpets so I knew then she was ill. Mess like this would have been cleaned instantly.

I lifted her into the car and drove to the emergency room in the next town.

I continued to carry her until they found her a bed. I had just got my wife back I didn't want to loose her. I panicked as I saw the blood trickle through her lounging pants. I tried not to show my concern but I'm sure she saw the scared in my eyes.

A nurse took me by the arm seeing my face whiten and showed me to a waiting room.

"We will do everything to save them sir." she said.

I put my head in my hands. *Did she say them?*

Puzzled I leaned to look out the window towards Annie's bay. Machinery was being wheeled in but the curtains were closed. I knew she would be scared but she knew also if there was blood I would be useless.

It seemed forever when they wheeled Annie to a ward and came to see me. A young doctor entered and I tried not to think about which parts of my wife's body he had been seeing, touching. I felt myself begin to rage, no-one touches my wife.

"Annie is fine Mr Turner but I am afraid we lost one of the babies."

What did he just say? Bab_ies_? I didn't know about one let alone plural. His statement calmed my anger with confusion.

"Its a more common problem in identical twins than you'd think. One gave way to the other, natures way of providing one healthy baby rather than two at risk. Mr Turner, how far along was your wife? Second trimester?"

I racked my brain. "I...I don't know, I mean, we didn't know. We didn't know she was pregnant." he looked at me in amazement.

"I'm sorry for the shock Mr Turner. Your wife was in pain so we gave her some gas and air and she was slipping in and out of consciousness so we never got to establish the facts with her. She is resting now. She will be sleepy for a while but you can go to her side. There is a midwife here to come and sit with you to explain and if you have any problems." With that he got up to leave and the midwife sat in his place. "My condolences Mr Turner. We were able to see the sex of the baby if it helps you to come to terms with your lose?" I nodded, "He was a boy. Your wife is carrying a girl. Er... Congratulations" and she too left.

The midwife thought Annie was around five months. Our daughter looked healthy as she had fought for her brothers nutrients and lived off him. I panged at the thought of him suffering but how brave to allow his sister the life they should have shared together. Then a thought crept into my head - how was I going to tell Annie? We had never wanted children. Choosing luxuries in life over nappies and vomit but hearing how our daughter had fought, at any cost, to be born I now just wanted to hold her. Tell her everything was going to be alright, wasn't that what daddy's did?

"A baby Annie, we're going to have a baby!" I couldn't think of an easy way to say it as Annie awoke on a over warm ward full of other women. The décor was more pleasant than the room I had been shown to with its nylon fabric covered chairs that had seen no doubt hundreds of bottoms and rivers of emotion. I had pulled the nearly translucent threadbare floral curtains around us meeting every visitors eye in the process. I knew they would be on the other side now wondering what the need for privacy was. Annie starred at me, thinking I was mad no doubt. She had come in here earlier one person feeling ill and now she was going to be a mum. I think I baffled her and myself because I couldn't remember the things I needed to tell her, the science bits.

I walked away to get the midwife I had spoken to earlier and give Annie some time. After I'd shown her the sonogram she went into denial. I guess being shown a picture of something that is growing inside you could freak you out a little. When I returned, unfortunately without the midwife who had finished her shift, Annie was sat up in bed.

"We're going to do this." she said and for the first time in what seemed like forever we kissed. A long slow meaningful kiss. The kind that warms you from the inside and made me look to the future.

Over the next couple of weeks we told people

our news. Firstly about our son who we decided to name Jacob. We watched their faces fall with sadness and then raise again as we told them about Bella. I had wanted to name her Annabel, the same as her mum. Our little bundle had fought to survive and the most courageous and strong woman I know is my wife. Annie didn't agree with my reasoning but liked a shortened 'Bella', so we agreed it would be Annabel on her birth certificate, and Bella for short.

I flung myself whole heartily into the pregnancy even surprising Annie with tickets to 'The Baby Show', I'd seen on The Apprentice. I don't think she enjoyed it as much as me but then I could run freely from stall to stall and she would have to waddle! Also the hall was full of expectant mothers with their own mothers and Annie being with me and having no mum of her own to bring I think made her sad all over again.

We managed a weekend away before Bella would arrive. Edinburgh was welcoming and the relaxing time we had before the hectic future was good for Annie. She spent her days relaxing by the pool and swimming. She liked the way swimming made her feel weightless even with a bump. We had our photo taken besides a tall dark wooden, beautiful fireplace, our last memory as a twosome. No doubt we would age fast once Bella arrived and by the time she turned 18 and we could relax again she would have caused a lifetime of concern, activities and worry-lines.

To have Annie to myself that weekend was wonderful. To all around we were a happy couple expecting a bundle and I guess we were. Though every so often my mind would wonder towards my past and the realisation I had tarnished it with a dirty Jenny interlude that I could never delete.

The last slog before Bella arrived was the hardest for Annie. She would freak out every morning with nothing to wear and stand in front of the mirror for ages trying to look over her shoulder and see what she looked like from behind. She loved that she could eat whatever she liked but hated the prospect of giving everything up she had got used to again once there was no reason to be larger than her 'normal'. Work wise she was coping fine. I was pleased when Time gave Annie time off then a structured return pattern after our initial shock. We hadn't sat down and spoke about when her maternity leave finished but as far as I was concerned she was leaving procedures for a replacement as I was positive I didn't want her returning to work post birth. They had yet to find a suitable candidate so Annie spent the last 3 weeks bored much preferring to scan the internet for last minute purchases than reading a new script or archiving her procedures.

I watched her wonder in today, her last day. Laden down with well wishers gifts of cute something's they couldn't resist in every shade of pink imaginable. She was in her element, centre of attention and I would keep in my office at the end of the hall watching her lap up the final work hours before she could finally get in the mind set to mother my child growing in her tummy.

Jenny had been funny once the grapevine rumours were confirmed that me and Annie were expecting. With the drama of finding out the way we did it had obviously captured everyone's attention and whenever I entered the building between hospital visits it was in reception they collared me for details and reception was Jenny's territory. She has showed no emotion when she overheard me speak of Jacob. She even tried to blackmail me into starting back on again or she'd tell Annie. The idea was comical but I couldn't risk my happy future and thankfully admin was within my budget so a pay rise was enough of a breathing space until I figured out what I was to do. Not once did I consider starting our affair again but I wondered whether telling Annie would be the way forward. I went back and forth on the idea, finally resulting that if it was the opposite I would never forgive her so I kept quiet telling Jenny that Annie knew. I took a gamble she wouldn't bring it up, after all Annie could gloat I chose her and not Jenny so why would Jenny want the embarrassment?

It had been months since Jenny had come into my office but in she burst now, not sexily as in months past but panicked and out of breath.

"Annie... blood, toilets!" she panted and paced back to reception as I followed her hastily.

What had this women done? Blood? Had she stabbed my wife? What was she talking about?

As I pasted reception I caught the conversation Jenny was having on the phone 'Yes ambulance please' she was saying. *Was she dialling 999?*

The situation became apparent when I opened the door to the ladies that Jenny pointed me to. There was Annie and her waters, tinged with a lot of fresh red blood, on the floor.

I put my arms out to her. We both spoke over each other as I lifted her out down to the path and waited for the ambulance which I could hear approaching in the distance. Thankfully I didn't have time to panic even with blood on my shoes.

Once inside we rocked along as the ambulance sped us to hospital. I wanted to reassure Annie, I wanted to hold her hand she was offering and place it with her other on Bella's bump, but I couldn't. I sat with my head in my hands praying for a miracle, praying my girls would be safe.

As I held her close on the way down to neonatal unit I couldn't take my eyes off her. The last hour had been the scariest of my life and now I held new life in my arms. Annie had had to have a c-section because of the emergency but thankfully the procedure was done under local rather than general anaesthetic so she was awake to see Bella arrive. There had been a few tense moments whilst she took her first few breaths but holding her now she was perfect. Her lips were so big on her face and her eyes, wow, they were going to break hearts when she was older. Annabel 'Bella' Turner had arrived, amongst panic and tears but safely.

I had managed to show off our girl to Annie as she lay on the bed still being sewn up. I lay Bella on her chest and watched Annie's eyes fill with tears.

They had wrapped her up well and Annie was right when she said goodbye, she did look like an Eskimo hiding from the cold.

Day after day I visited them both. Bella was allowed out of neonatal unit after 24 hours and remained with Annie in hospital. It was great seeing them but leaving them everyday was hard. I had got used to sleeping with Annie besides me again and now every night she wasn't there. I didn't really know Bella either. I could go in and see her everyday, but only Annie fed her and she slept most of the time. I wanted them home to start our new life properly.

At two weeks old I got the news I had waited for, Bella was well enough to come home. I didn't have long to organise it but I wanted people at home to welcome my girls so I gave my sister our house keys and some money for cakes and drinks.

I had been into work on a couple of occasions, saving my paternity leave for when we could be all home together. The days in the office were not very productive, me and Annie working in the same company meant all wanted to know about everything. I found myself stuck in the kitchen a few hours a day simply replaying Bella's dramatic entrance whilst trying to make a 'quick' coffee. At first it was hard, after all the kitchen backs onto reception and that's where Jenny sits but then after I had done it a few times it was easy to forget my ex life with her and it was hard to remember a time when Bella didn't exist. To think we hadn't ever planned for her sent chills down my spine.

On the day they were discharged I popped into the office to see HR. I had to leave a note as no-one was there personally, requesting my leave to start today and to do some housekeeping on my PC.

The journey to pick them up was exciting. I set my mind to daddy-mode, I guessed for the next 18 years! I smiled; curb-side they waited. Bags of belongings we had slowly bought in but never brought home again. The newest and most special bundle was secured in first and Annie climbed in next to her. She still looked so small to have had such an impact.

It was a slow journey home. Every bend seemed like a 90 degree angle and every stone felt like a speed bump. It was the first time I had ever felt restless in Annie's chunky and massive 4x4. It was the perfect cell to hold them in away from the careless drivers and ridiculous speed limits that I myself undertook daily. To think the outside with its influence and stupidness was only inches from her had all but turned me into Mr Roadsafe himself. Bella was so beautiful, so precious and mine. I still couldn't believe it. Women all over the world must learn how to ask for the world in the days after giving birth, any man would feel so unimportant compared to making him a dad. There is nothing that we could give the fairer sex that would compare. I had never been so happy. With my precious cargo aboard we drove to start our new life.

Annie was surprised at the turn out at our house. My sister had done an amazing job, offering pink cakes, pink drinks and pink 'Its A Girl' balloons. We toasted with pink champagne as our daughter lay in her moses basket. I took the kind presents up to the nursery but something caught my eye in our gym, the door, it was ajar. I never leave the door open, years of nagging, it had become habit to close it. Annie thought the machines were bulky and the odour seething from there showed it was used often!

I lent in to simply close the door and there spread across my weights bench was Jenny! *Shit.* Bizarrely with an envelop between her lips instead of the more customary rose.

"What the hell are you doing here?" I spurned in hushed tones, "Get out!" I grabbed her by the arm, she tried to fight and the envelop fell to the floor. I could clear that later, right now had to get her out.

"I got your note." she said as I got her to the stair well.

"What note?" I was baffled and panicked my eyes darting everywhere for watchers.

"That you'd be home today, thanks for letting me know you'd not be in work for a few weeks. I think keeping 'us' away from work is a great idea and with Annie stuck at home with the kid now it'll be easy."

"What are you talking about? The note was to HR. I don't want you Jenny. I have a family. I am happy, something one day I hope you find but not with me. Now get out." I finally got her downstairs.

I closed all the doors upstairs and followed her. She went straight for Annie. As I watched from the galleried landing she sat next to her on our sofa infecting my scene of happiness. Was my life about to change drastically again for the third time this year?

After a brief conversation Annie got up and left Jenny alone, I thought she'd leave. *Was she waiting for the bombshell ricochet?* Annie had looked worried and disappeared into the kitchen. I watched her go, *was she looking for me*? I needed to find out. By the time I reached the bottom step Jenny had left out the front door, quietly, only noticed by me. I hurried to the kitchen. I hugged

Annie, she let me, she didn't finch. Was she still mine?

I improvised and asked Annie to say goodbye to the visitors, she looked tired. The last of them left and we were finally alone, just the three of us.

I nuzzled into Annie on the sofa. God knows what Jenny had said to her but things were fine. Annie was still welcoming to me. She seemed edgy but having your bundle home for the first time was nervy. I cleared up as she dozed for five minutes on the sofa. I wanted a turn in the gym so thought I'd take Bella up to the nursery to give Annie longer shut eye once she'd finished feeding her.

As I walked up the stairs cradling my daughter I looked from Annie to Bella and back again. They shared the same vivid blond hair and nose. My life was complete, two beautiful girls to look after for life.

I opened the door to my gym after pulling myself from Bella's cot side. She was so tiny in there. I knew time would fly and she'd be answering me back and climbing up the drainpipes at all hours before I knew it but right now she was silent.

The machinery buzzed on and as it took a few moments to re-boot I changed into my shorts and tee. Bending down to put on my trainers I noticed the envelop Jenny had brought in but dropped during our struggle. Knowing her it was probably some pornographic photos of her to get to me. I'd better check before throwing them into the bin.

Inside there weren't photos but eleven pieces of paper. Bizarrely Jenny had brought what looked like work to the party. The first sheet was Annie's expenses for the weekend she was away in June, interviewing in London. Maybe Annie hadn't claimed the travel or something?

I flicked through them, the rest were emails from Annie's work account. On the day Bella was born I had heard Annie ask Jenny to turn her PC off, maybe these were her unfinished works?

Though work emails shouldn't contain kisses, I thought seeing all the 'xxx' beneath.

As I flicked thought them again I had to sit. These were from a guy to my wife. I read and re-read and had to go back time and time again to understand. With each page turned my disbelief boiled into anger. This guy wasn't only craving my wife he had had her, in London, on *that* weekend. He spoke like he was in love with her, no wait, he was in love with her. I quote, 'I love you with every bone in my body'. *Bastard.*

Then the knife really stuck in - Bella. He was questioning Bella. *My daughter.* My mathematics towards pregnancy weren't great especially when I was so flustered, but June till February, yes, Bella had been 3 weeks early too.

The dates matched.

I raged as I heard Bella cry. A sound that would

normally of filed me with worry, but this time it only raised my anger.

I heard Annie coming up the stairs.

Could this be, could the guy on these pages, be ruining my life? Had he ruined it months ago? Taking my family dreams and in eleven pages stolen it from me for himself?

But Annie was still here, what was happening? I had to ask her. I was beginning to hate her. The thought of another mans hands on her but if there was any chance Bella was mine she'd have a fight on her hands.

I walked along the landing and heard Annie lift Bella out of her cot. I opened the door silently just a pinch, 'Let me tell you about your *real* daddy' I heard her whisper.

A haze descended over my eyes. They were gone, my wife, my baby and my dreams. I flung the door open ignoring the aching pain running through my heart and seeing nothing but betrayal, humiliation and a stranger who I once loved.

"That would be good!" I shouted at her.

At first Annie spun round scared and surprised. I was screaming at her, lines from the emails in my hand, asking what the hell was going on. What she thought she was doing?

She had the audacity to reply, "What's going on?"

I flipped, "What's going on you slut is that you've been found out. You and your dirty secret. Get out" I raised my arms, "GET OUT".

"You're scaring Bella" she said.

Like I bloody care, "I don't care what I'm doing to that, that bastard baby of Yours!"

She ran past me. Probably for the best, I had been walking towards her getting closer and closer and to be honest, with my anger raging I wasn't sure what I would do if I had reached her. The baby cried. I threw the emails at her, it was that or a fist at this point.

She grabbed one. I turned away afraid of what I might do next. She had to leave now. Only my eyes met a t-shirt my sister had brought, 'my daddy loves me' it smirked on a teddy sized piece of cloth. I threw it at her, screaming as the tears came to my eyes and the lump hit my throat.

What happened next will re-play in my mind in slow motion for as long as I live. Annie and Bella tumbled backwards, down the stairs, rolling and rolling from stair to banister, crashing this way and that.

I ran down after them, Oh My God.

It was an accident but who would believe that. I had to think fast, the spark in Annie's eyes had gone and her eye lids closed, there were puddles of blood around her head. Bella started to cry, there too was blood on her ear but as I looked closer it had splashed from Annie. Bella appeared to have landed on her bag, that I now assume Annie had packed to run to him with. Had it formed a cushion? I picked Bella up and with some TLC she stopped crying and sucked her fist. I fished for her dummy and placed her in her moses basket. Could it be, could she be fine and Annie gone?

I looked at Annie and realised she needed medical attention. I dialled 999 and asked for an ambulance. I gave the address and hung up. I didn't know what I was doing but I grabbed the car seat, Bella's bag, the car keys and Bella and I left Annie and our house in the rear view mirror.

As I sped down our street I passed the ambulance speeding in the opposite direction up our road and to my ex-house and ex-wife.

The only person who knew Bella wasn't mine was laying in a pool of her own blood at the bottom of a staircase. I could have Bella, I clutched back at my dreams. Just me and her and the open road.

Our journey took us north of the village. I needed to think where I was going and Bella would need a feed. I pulled over and as the engine went off Bella's eyes opened. I reached over to get the map and my stomach flipped and my heart ached. I hung my head, with a single flash of her eyes she had shown me where I needed to go.

It was a normal suburban street, quiet and neat, especially given its location to London. I knocked on the door. I realised I didn't even know his name, his emails were signed with 'X's and one bizarrely as 'Eskimo'. This I guessed was a pet name between them and I realised then they had history. I remembered back to the maternity theatre and Annie calling Bella an Eskimo, I had been a fool for long enough. I rang the doorbell. I needed to get out of here but I needed to meet him. *Was it a guy thing?* I wondered, I needed to see who had stolen my wife and would be raising her daughter.

He opened the door, tousled hair, Bella's plump lips, and tired but definitely Bella's eyes. I didn't know how this was going to go. Under it all I guessed my reactions so far showed I had cared about this little girl and I had to be strong not angry during this exchange.

To say I was surprised when he offered me his hand and showed me into his home with a, 'you must be Andy' would be an understatement. This guy knew who I was and was so pleasant. I had only just found out he existed but he knew me as Annie's husband and that made the whole thing more sordid for me. I wanted to ask him about it but his eyes fell. I don't think he was looking for Annie he had in fact seen Bella in her car seat.

I didn't say anything when he undid her belt and pulled her out. Maybe I didn't need to. He himself had know Bella was his from his emails. Bella nestled in the crook of his arm, she was home.

I stood to leave. I hadn't said a word.

"And Annie?" he asked.

I had delivered him a daughter, a daughter not yesterday I considered my own, did he really think I would deliver my wife too?

"It was her final wishes," I lied "for her daughter to be with her true father."

"Final wishes?" he sat down "She's really gone." his voice quivered. "I had a dream last night she had died. I dreamt her saying goodbye to me."

With that I left, perhaps they did have a connection like his emails quoted. I pulled his front door open to a click but with resistance as he was pulling it back open.

Puzzled he looked at me, "Her names Bella - Annabel." I said. How did this guy do it. I didn't know him, yet I could tell he was going to be a good dad. "Her birthday is the 29th February."

Now I *was* leaving. Firstly to the hospital - with Annie there I needed to see whether she was in fact dead or alive. I had decided to tell him she was gone. I didn't want him looking for her. The last thing I wanted to picture was them playing happy families in the years to come.

Things were definitely over between Annie and I if she was alive. I hated her. My life had changed indescribably within these 24 hours and it was all due to her. Dead or alive, I didn't care. There was something evil in hoping she was alive so I could tell her Bella was dead.

As I lay my wedding band next to a comatosed Annie and on top of a reality check note I took deep breath. I had a lot to do before Annie woke, if she woke? She was alive for now, barley, breathing through machines.

To steal everything away from her would be my mission. To leave her with nothing, as I am now, nothing to live for. Ripping her heart out as she realised everything and everyone had gone would be justice for breaking mine.

In the fresh air of the car park I clicked open my car, jumped in and wondered, with the world at my feet, what my clean sheet life could hold.

A thought popped into my head. I started the engine and grinned - *I wonder what Jenny is up to this evening?*

FIVE

As I kissed Annie outside the generic coffee shop at Victoria station I knew this was going to be harder than I thought. Since we met years ago we have always gravitated towards each other every couple of years. Now, with age perhaps, I was scared that what we shared was a connection and as we continued kissing I needed to understand the reasons we always found not to be together and smash them out of our minds.

I wanted it to be like our second day. The first was good but full of nerves and newness and the second, Wow. I remember my lips were numb by the end of the day. We were having to say goodbye the following morning as I had taken me so long to approach her during the college Artic Experience trip. I truly felt I knew everything about her as we parted. I guess we'll never know what we missed about the Eskimos that day but I figured I had a whole lifetime to get to know my own Eskimo.

I have always been confident around this woman from our first meet where within a couple of days of noticing her and a couple of minutes of actually meeting her I had her pinned against a door. The stolen weekends that have punctured our history, in between relationships, there is just something confident about knowing you are liked and there was no question she liked me. I wasn't used to the thrill of it all. I don't know where the confidence came from the first time but the sparkle in her eyes ever since and the way she can never hold my gaze for too long without looking down and giggling. No matter how old now she remained that 18 year old flushed with a first crush attitude whenever she invited me in. Many men say it is 'the chase' that turns them on but for me its her, everything about Annie.

She is beautiful, intelligent, she fights back and makes me laugh. She is blunt and sassy and I needed to know on this meet why she wasn't mine - permanently.

I was going into this weekend with my mind fully on winning her. I finally wanted to taste a relationship with her not continue years of flirting and missed opportunities.

I had tended to contact Annie between relationships for some harmless flirting and dodgy emails but our distance, professions and life styles had meant we had never actually got it together, reasons that now seemed ridiculous looking at her over her coffee cup which had carrot cake frosting around the rim. After a lot of sole searching my efforts were going towards winning this lady, this weekend and for keeps.

It was when Annie had disappeared into the lift at the hotel to drop off her ridiculous sized suitcase when the feeling of 'this is it' and 'now or never' clichés hit me. I raced up the stairs. Two at a time not over thinking my actions for fear of embarrassment. I heard the door click and knew she was hidden inside behind the beech effect laminated door of this west London hotel chain. I waited outside for her to come out, take her by surprise. I panted, partly catching breath from the run up the flights and partly in anticipation. The door opened.

She tasted incredible. Once again Mr Confident had taken over and pinned her against the wall. She hungrily kissed me back. My boxers automatically became tight with her heavy breathing and thoughts of what might happen as she easily let me undress her. Her breasts were heaving in gorgeous lingerie, her heart pounding making them larger with every breath. I cupped them, kissing them and ran my hands over her pert nipples. She arched her back in pleasure and it was like a green light to me, this Mr Confident was good but Annie wanted Me. She slowly lowered her palm under my briefs elastic after releasing me of all my clothes except them. *Dare I sigh and enjoy or should I concentrate on her?* I thought as my eyes rolled upwards towards the ceiling and stretched out the desire she was pumping into me.

Bang bang bang
WTF! Who the hell was that?
She stopped.
"Ms Turner, security, is everything alright? Reception said they saw a man run up the stairs in your direction?"

This wasn't a time for humour but she was making me laugh. I wasn't going to let some intruders steel our moment but she continued to answer their questions through the door so I slowly knelt down. My fingers scrapping the inside of her thigh then my tongue followed its path, higher, higher, she whimpered, and higher into her insides.

*Ouch! S*he pulled my head backwards with a fist of my hair. The situation had got to her, she yanked me up, face-to-face. Her eyes yearning - I lifted her up, wrapping her legs around me and entered her. Her eyes rolled now and the conversation through the door was over. We thrust hard, kissing rampantly and continued to do so until the end euphoric hurdle was breached simultaneously.

Through panting I broke away from our gentle lip brushing, "Why haven't we done that before!"

There have been a few occasions where passions have reached breaking point but we had never indulged. Once in our early meets we were asked to move from a park where we had taken a picnic, as we ate more of each other than the food we had packed!

Another time, my favourite memory, when Annie was bored during a 'Super Sunday' Sky viewing when I had gone to stay at her new flat-share. She had leaned in to kiss me, I obliged until kissing turned to snogging and snogging got heavy and cheers came from the match. Women are wrong when they say men cannot multitask, until that point I had easily engaged Annie and kept an open eye on the football! Unfortunately I earned myself a playful slap and she took her lips away when she noticed.

And other times we have always just enjoyed being together. There had been touching and closeness but perhaps it was because we always knew it was temporary and sex would confuse things further. I cannot talk for Annie but parting all these times messed me up for a good few weeks afterwards. Annie was infectious and now I wanted to be totally quarantined.

It was afternoon when we got ourselves off that hotel bed. Laying together afterwards was just what I needed, to feel Annie was totally here with me.

Now though it was evening and we were walking the streets holding hands after a few, then a few more, drinks. Maybe it was the alcohol softening my male pride but I continued to want a lifetime of this. I was angry at myself for not coming to this conclusion earlier. The wasted years but maybe I needed all those other years, for maturity, for experience and to realise what love really was. Yes, I was in no doubt, I loved this lady in my hand.

I wondered if she knew how I felt about her, I wondered if she felt the same. I had wooed her for years but she had always left. I needed something special. I pulled her backwards catching her as she slipped off the edge of the fountain she was balancing on and fell towards me. I met her eyes. It could have been ten years ago as she looked at me, her eyes hadn't changed. Squeezing her waist I held her, my confidence bubbling up inside. I wanted to blurt it all out. Say I never wanted her to leave, and, oh, just to tell her I love her but as she starred back I broke away. *What if she didn't want that? What if this was just another stolen weekend? What If...?*

My hands lowered and eyes dropped as the doubt set in.

"Annie?" I was going to ask her outright but my fingers brushed a ridge, "What are you hiding under there?".

From the moment I felt that I knew. She didn't need to run away like she did and all the time I chased her, slowly - playing the game - I smiled. Under her dress was a present for me - an intimate present. We were going to be together again and if Annie had planed it then she wanted it too. Forget the What Ifs, I had her, or more over, she was going to have me!

I never pictured her as a fantasist but she was rampant. She formed a blindfold out of my t-shirt she had just striped me of, and out of pure astonishment I let her put it over my eyes not worrying what a state I would look like tomorrow with all the creases!

She was slow and thoughtful, taking care of every item of clothing and caressing the place that had just been revealed. Running her hand up my trousers legs I finally started to consider ripping off the blindfold and grabbing her but she left the bed and when I next felt her near she was eye popping. My eyes wondered all over her skin, which bit would I start with? She had to place my hands herself as I was mesmerised.

Tongues lashing and hands wondering everywhere, she still wouldn't let me in and before I could protest the blindfold was replaced and I had something else to worry about. She was kissing my chest and getting lower and lower, I didn't want to ruin this, she was on a mission and every part of me was hoping my elation, and sperm levels could stay intact long enough!

Oh Christ, she took me in her mouth, long licks from the bottom to the tip. How was she doing this, how was I not exploding. I had to thrust.

Then she stopped! My fingers were guided past her silk into warm, moist depths. I wanted to make her shudder.

She mounted me and I delved deep inside her. I lifted my groin in the air and stretched in pleasure.

Wow this woman was getting better as time went on. I rolled to her, rubbing noses like the Eskimos we had come to know each other as, we were close physically and mentally, closer than ever.

"I love you." I whispered into her lips.

I waited.

The air had disappeared around me, my lungs struggling and my heart aching. For Annie had not said the words I'd expected but she had in one swoop, crushed me, 'I'm married' she'd responded.

With her words Annie had rolled over to the edge of the bed. Stunned and laying still, I racked my brains I couldn't think of an easy way forward now. My mission this weekend would now surely fail. I stared up to the ceiling. I think Annie was asleep, she twitched as her body closed down into rest mode.

She was so close but so far away. Within reach but not mine. Memories of our stolen weekends flew in and out of my mind. The amount of times I had rekindled contact with a cheeky 'Eskimo Calling?' text or email and we would easily find each other again.

On a boys holiday to Ibiza, intoxicated, I still knew her figure dancing on that bar top. Hundreds of miles away from home and we ended up in the same bar.

Me and the boys had our 'pull-chart' that

holiday, pride of place on the rented apartment wall. I disappointed them by receiving only 1 star next to my name that holiday, meeting Annie on night number two and remaining next to her until our plane departed five nights later.

That had been an amazing time. We'd walk back from the clubs at 4am, she'd be barefoot negotiating obstacles on the path because her high, expensive, fashionable shoes were a nightmare to actually walk in! Some nights I'd carry her home when the alcohol had not been her friend and some nights we'd sing and dance on the streets both relaxed not just from the cocktail intake but the company of each other. We had passionately kissed the night I first spotted her on that bar top. I tapped her on the leg which was on my eye level, she looked down and jumped! We didn't speak a word only rubbing noses before our lips locked together, we abandoned our friends and walked out. Not till we found a spot on the sand did we say 'hello'. Mostly staring at each other in disbelief that we were on the same island, smiling cheesy, happy grins that said a million words and sharing sensational kisses.

The sun had rose and it felt like we'd been there a lifetime. Along with the stragglers we walked the streets home. That is my favourite meet with Annie.

Other nights things had got hot and heavy but sharing an apartment with four friends each we never indulged. We hung back sometimes, pining one another on the sand and rolling around but honestly it just never happened. Its like we didn't want to ruin it. The holiday was perfect but we knew we would still be catching separate planes and returning to our own normality. Maybe sex was an extra complication we couldn't handle.

Now Annie breathed heavily in the pitch black that awashed the hotel room. Sleeping seemed hard with all these thoughts racing around but around 4am they did take me off to the land of nod where no doubt anxiety filled dreams would pour into my subconscious.

Sunlight streamed through the windows and I rolled towards her thinking freshly about last nights revelation. I had decided I would also come clean. I had played over every conversation and they all ended with us parting. Annie would wake feeling awkward. I know her and she would be panicking about our first encounter this morning. With that in mind I rolled to her, wrapping my arm over her shoulder and gently pulled her towards me.

Eventually she rolled to me but placed her hand over her face, a barrier. I looked at her, though I had decided honesty was best I couldn't look at her whilst I said it.

"I'm married too!" I squeezed out.

I had removed my wedding ring on the drive from home. Home was pleasant but I wanted out. This wasn't a rash decision upon contacting Annie again. My wife, Lizzy, and I had been married for 2 years. She had cheated on me just before the wedding but too scared to let 'the family' down and knowing the pennies that had been spent I was pushed into going ahead, up the aisle and into a trust-less marriage. She had tried since but once there is doubt there really is no point. My marriage was over in every sense but Annie had seemed guilty with her revelation, *did she want to be married?* I had to ask.

To my surprise she laughed whilst leaning in to kiss me. Gob smacked I couldn't react. Had she heard me? Did she care? But then I knew she had just relaxed as I had taken some of the guilt.

Finally I kissed her back.

I knew we weren't going to exchange wedding stories. I knew as our gentle kissing turned more intense that this would be the last time. Then I knew I didn't have to ask, in a few hours I'd finally let her go.

We made love slowly, longingly, looking into each others eyes throughout. It wasn't about pleasure it was about getting the closest we could in the time we had left.

I wanted to hold onto her and never leave that room. We had had our time and it was the perfect way to say goodbye. I heard her leave quietly. I couldn't find the right words so I lay still and let he rub her nose on mine and I took in her scent, a fragrance that needed to last me a lifetime.

SIX

I listened to my voice mail on my journey home. Mine nor Annie's mobiles had made a sound all weekend. Mine had been switched off in my coat pocket, a coat I hadn't needed because of the weather and therefore I didn't feel it banging against my chest, with every step pumping guilt inwards for turning it off.

I had three messages.

The first was from Lizzy asking to call. Politely, normally.

The second from Lizzy. More excitedly maybe, asking me to call.

The third, Lizzy, CALL ME PLEASE.

With the tarmac speeding under the car and the white lines flicking past the wheels it made for easy mind wondering. Annie had gone and now I knew I had to give myself a break. Lizzy had cheated on me and now I had her, no matter how we tried it wasn't working I think of all the people who will be disappointed but surely whether they're disappointed or not they'd want Lizzy and

I to be happy; and with each other that wasn't happening.

I didn't call Lizzy back. Telling someone you want out of a marriage, a divorce I guess, deserved face-to-face at the least.

I parked outside the house, not on the drive. I didn't know which one of us would be leaving the house and if it was in anger on Lizzy's part I didn't want to block her car in. I thought she'd leave as she has places she could stay however maybe hearing I no longer wanted to be married to her and expecting her to leave Our house was a bit much.

I opened the door and she flew at me, not angry, extremely happy. It was like I was returning from war not a weekend away. Before I could drop my rucksack she jumped onto me, wrapping her legs around my waist and grinning, grinning widely. OK, I had to ask, "What's up?"

I looked towards the living room, there was bags of new stuff everywhere, perhaps we'd won the lottery? I thought her sister must have been visiting because between all the shopping bags were kids toys and nappies and wipes and bottles and all the other junk that comes with having children. Then I walked further into the room and saw a large flat pack cardboard box with the picture of a cot on the front.

Confused I turned around to ask her what kind of baby bomb had exploded in our lounge but she held her hands out like a plate and laying there was a small piece of plastic. I had never seen one before but I knew what it was. It was white, punctuated with two clear blue lines.

Lizzy screamed, "Its positive. We're having a baby, we're having a baby!" she danced around the living room chanting the words, *'we're having a baby, we're having a baby',* like a train speeds over and over its tracks, the words rattled in my head.

I sat down. She probably thought through amazement and she was right, I was amazed but mostly I was thinking I couldn't possibly leave her now.

"I didn't even know we were trying for a baby. I thought, call me old fashioned but I thought it was a joint venture?" Lizzy didn't like this, she stopped the dancing and chanting.

"Aren't you happy?" She asked, "When we met you said you wanted to be a daddy." This was true, I did want to be a dad, I would make a good daddy. I knew exactly what not to do from my own barely there father. She continued, "With everything that we have been through I thought a baby would be a good new start. Something exciting to join us together."

"Christ Lizzy, its not something you surprise a person with. Things have been awful here, you cant expect me to be pleased you've cheated me into it." She dropped to the sofa, I held out my hands. Raising them to the sky as if asking for help from above the clouds. "Yes I really want a baby, one day, but I think a child should come into a happy and secure environment. Its all going way over my head, I mean a baby, *my baby,* is in there." I sat and placed my hand to her tummy, "How can I get my head around that?"

She kissed me on my temple as I continued to stare at her belly. She knew I would come round, she knew I wanted a baby and she had tricked me but I would never hold it against her. It was true that a baby needed all those things I had mentioned and I knew running all this through my head this baby would be born and loved more than anything I had ever experienced.

Good god I was going to be a dad! The male ego and pride in me glowed. I was continuing to a new generation. I had impregnated another. One of my guys had swam like a salmon towards the goal of Life.

I pictured the opening credits of 'Look Who's Talking' and my one mighty guy crossing the finishing line. My chest puffed out slightly - I had done it. Me and my sperm were Life Makers!

Though Lizzy had planned on this she wasn't as up on conceiving as she thought. As she lay on the couch in the scanning room we found out actually that things were a lot closer than we thought. Going privately we had requested a scan the soonest we could and only a week since finding out we were expecting we were told our baby was four months gestation and he was a boy. So as it turned out Lizzy's shopping spree had been a good thing and we were prepared well. We could continue to add blue purchases to the stash and buy these *together*.

It wasn't a lie when I said I was happy. I was so excited at the prospect of becoming a father. My mind had erased any thoughts of leaving when Lizzy delivered the news and although our situation wasn't ideal I knew I would be a good dad for my son and that was all that counted right now. Even if I hadn't been sure seeing him bounce around the screen today, hearing his heartbeat and naming him would have pushed me over the excitement barrier should I have needed it.

The news came as a shock to my mum. I'm very close to my mum and she knew of my intentions with Lizzy. She also knew all about Annie, from start to present. From an 18 year old excited lad returning from a boring Artic college trip. Having bagged a girl that set the smile on my face all summer long; to the last meet where I had finally had to let her go.

I decided to tell mum alone. I wanted to tell her how it felt loosing Annie and having to look forward again. She was supportive and told me everyone has doubts in life. The scene didn't start well. I sat to tell her and she had the usual 'Magic' radio station playing all the old smooching songs. 'Finally Found' by the Honeyz filled the lounge as tears filled my eyes before I could open my mouth. It was our song, mine and Annie's.

The goodbye with Annie had sunk my heart to a low. My mum knew it always took me awhile to bounce back to normality after seeing her but now it was for real. A 'goodbye' not a 'see you soon'. I was only tormenting myself mum said switching stations. The weekend had never been forgotten as my sons existence had jumped onto the memory and into the void left by Annie.

My dad entered the room as we started to talk about Lizzy's growing bump. Dad was in disbelief that Lizzy could have already been pregnant when she decided she should try and get pregnant. A missed period made her question whether she was but then the idea of being a mummy had took over and she began to try!

My history with my dad wasn't good but we had a good relationship now. He used to work a lot and when he did have the day off on a Sunday he would sleep late, watch the football, motor GP or cricket - which ever the season. The weekday evenings he would come home when I was asleep and Sundays he would go for a whiskey with his own dad. A man I barely knew, except that he told me his wife, my dads mum had ran off to Canada with a neighbour just before I was born!

My childhood past by 'fatherless' and by the time he wanted me in his life I had discovered girls, beer and late nights myself.

It was mum I went to for Everything and it was mum who sat us both down when I was around 19. I was vulnerable emotionally from leaving

Annie at Trocadero in the afternoon on a flying visit from her before her flight left out of Heathrow. Mum thought my mind set would enable me to be frank with dad, and it did.

We decided over tea and malt loft that we wouldn't hold the past against our future and the following Sunday we were at the away end of White Hart Lane as my team were in town.

Lizzy and I went to baby show after baby show, buying every latest gadget and money making scheme related to first born babies. Where the parents are naive and will buy anything for their bundle. Time was slipping slowly by and Lizzy and I were friends again. We didn't sleep together, Lizzy had gotten huge and though I had mentioned it she found herself self conscious and the logistics difficult. By the time our son was due we were contented in our relationship, wondering everyday about what our baby will look like, who he would take after. Would he be a mummies boy or independent and football playing son with his dad? Towards the end of the pregnancy, Lizzy was experiencing a lot of pain and the midwives were finding high levels of protein and blood in her samples, which she was having to do daily. Eventually they called her condition pre-eclampsia and admitted her for induction. This meant I could be there from the start so I was happy however it also meant it could be a long delivery and Lizzy would suffer until our son was born.

We arrived at the hospital early, 7:30am. We were strangely admitted to a ward where ladies were coming back from giving birth so had their babies waiting to leave. Thankfully due to my raging work offers we were able to afford private care so we were soon moved to a private side room with our own bathroom and Sky TV! In there we spread out all of Lizzy's packed and re-packed labour bag. She had thought of everything including magazines and snacks for me though my work papers filled most of the gaps in which Lizzy slept. The company I had pledged my 5 year allegiance to after Uni until next Christmas weren't the caring family firm allowing time for parenthood and had written an escape clause for me to take now that work wasn't my main priority. Solicitors were always needed and in this climate I was thinking about starting alone once this new chapter of my life was experienced.

The pessary tablet was placed inside Lizzy about 10:30. I have to admit to going to get a coffee to warm the still wintry February air as they erected the sheets over her knees and began to explain things. As soon as I heard 'cervix' and saw a pair of rubber gloves I was out of there!

We were told that if nothing happened in six hours Lizzy would have another tablet, and then if nothing happened Lizzy would be given a drip and have her waters broken - *another coffee machine visit for me then!*

It felt like a long journey so far to this point

but it seemed like today and probably tomorrow would be time consuming too.

I did the normal fatherly thing and brought her water and generally, if I'm honest got a little bored whilst she got disorientated on gas and air. The end of the day came and I had to go home as delivery didn't seem to be occurring today.

A second pessary had been given after dinner time due to them being busy and with only mild pains coming to no pattern they decided to leave Lizzy overnight and try afresh as priority in the morning.

I left the hospital disheartened. I thought by the time I got into bed that night I would be a father but it wasn't to be today.

After a takeaway dinner of which Lizzy wouldn't agree, I took a long hot shower, wondering how different life would be tomorrow. I only just heard the phone and ran to catch the last ring. I knew it had to be about Lizzy as it was past midnight and no-one else would be so inconsiderate at that hour.

"You need to come in Now," said the hospital voice.

"How can things have happened so fast?" I was nervous and excited.

"As quick as you can Sir." And the line went dead.

I entered the labour suite still with wet hair

and slightly dishevelled at the 'as quick as you can' comment, I didn't want to miss the birth. I walked straight down the corridor to where I had left Lizzy not four hours earlier. A man in a white coat grabbed my arm and took me into another room. There were babies all around behind a glass screen, I wondered if I had missed it and tried to make out the name cards. The doctor sat opposite me and a midwife entered holding a small blue blanket. I stood up and looked down at him, the midwife offered me the baby.

I had missed it.

This was my son.

Tears filled my eyes as I looked at this perfect bundle I was holding. He had my navy eyes that were struggling to stay open because of the harsh hospital lights.

I had so many questions, how had this happened so quickly and why was I told to go home? I had missed my son being born, I wasn't the first person or probably the sixth person he saw in his life. Was he OK? He looked and smelled amazing and where was Lizzy?

As if picking up on all the questions flying around in my head, the doctor flipped his hand for the midwife to take the baby filled blanket away from me. I held him back. Why couldn't I have him? Where was he going? Where was Lizzy?

"Its OK," the midwife said sensing my fear "I'm just going to take him to the other side of this glass, for a lay down, he's had a busy day to you know.

The doctor wants a quick word anyhow." and she left the room with a warm nan-like comforting smile about her.

I smiled at the doctor. He clenched his fist together, "I'm afraid there is no easy way of telling you this sir. Your wife gave birth quite soon after you left. As you know she requested an epidural to get her through the night as the pains seemed to increase quite fast. When administering the anaesthetist noticed a lot of discharge and blood under your wife. We got your son out with forceps and assisted delivery hoping your wife's condition would improve after the birth as with most pre-eclampsia, however, unfortunately sir she never stopped bleeding and went into shock. We didn't have time to send her up to theatre and I am afraid we tried our best but we lost her after seven minutes of CPR." he stopped, hoping for a reprieve or sign from me, "You will be given help with your son sir, er... would you like to see your wife?"

I starred back at him. Within minutes I had got from being a new family of three to a widowed daddy of a newborn. How does something like this happen in this day and age and in a private establishment. How can a lady, a healthy young lady die giving birth in hospital? I stood up and starred blankly through the glass towards the babies, I saw him immediately, crying no-one comforting him. I left to get him. He was mine after all and shouldn't be apart from his daddy, or his mummy. Had Lizzy even met him? Had she seen him? Did she die never knowing what he looked like?

The midwife and the doctor both stood in front of me. I hadn't cried, I couldn't believe it enough to show any emotion. Then the doctor opened the door to what was Lizzy's labour suite and I saw her. I fell to the floor. She was covered over up to her neck with sheets, still naked underneath from giving life to our child. I sobbed, holding onto my son and my exploding head not taking the days events in. I didn't get it, I didn't want to believe it. I pulled myself up and into the room. She was still warm under my touch. What were you supposed to say in situations like this, goodbye? I love you? I chose to kiss her on her forehead and told her I would always look after our child. He would grow up knowing all about her and I would bring him up to be a proud and independent young man.

When I left the room with surreal truth I saw Lizzy's family in the room I had been taken into and saw their faces and emotion crack when the line was delivered that Lizzy was gone.

I brought my son home a few hours after his birth. There was no need for him to be there, motherless and in a nursery, he needed to be home and I needed to be with him. I had never experienced emotion like it. I was mourning the lose of my sons mother and excited by his birth I was confused. I hadn't felt this 'ying-yang' since my weekend in London and having to leave Annie, forever. Ahh Annie. My heart was heavy and the only person in the world I wanted to hold me and tell me everything would be OK was her. I really did have no reason not to contact her now. I needn't feel guilt about my wife. We had become friends in the end but we were not a couple. I chose not to tell her I loved her on her death bed because quite honestly, and cruelly, my heart had belonged to someone else since my weekend in London, probably even before then. I knew Annie was married and I had to respect her choice but I needed to know who had got her, what did the man look like, what did he do? Most of all did he treat her and love her as I longed too.

When we came home from London I had found Annie's work email address on the hotel booking form I had been given upon departure. It had spent months now being folded and hidden in my laptop bag. I opened my laptop, engaged our hotmail account and typed out the first thing that jumped into my head.

SUBJECT: ESKIMO CALLING?
I NEED TO SEE HIM, THE MAN YOU MARRIED.
I CANT SHAKE IT I NEED TO SEE THE MAN WHO KEEPS YOU FROM BEING MINE X
send

I sat there waiting for a reply that would

probably never come. She had moved on. For twenty minutes I told myself it was a mistake, then it popped up with a ping.

YOURS TOO X

I opened the attachment, the first was a younger Annie stood in a beautiful huge white gown with a wide smiling groom at her side. She looked amazing, my heart jumped at the sight of her though it hurt that she had sent me a wedding picture. Was it a reminder, 'Stay away, I'm married'. I opened the next and saw nothing but a pregnant Annie starring back.
ANNIE, YOU'RE PREGNANT? I replied.
No reply. 5 minutes. No reply.

The emails poured out of me now, every time a thought popped into my head I sent it.

ANNIE... IS IT MINE?, *send*
WHATEVER YOUR REPLY I'LL RESPECT IT, *send*
I KNOW YOU ANNIE, I KNOW THIS FEELING IM GETTING, *send*
THIS WILL EAT AT YOU, *send*
THIS WILL EAT AT ME, *send*

I sat looking at the screen but nothing came.

I know Annie wouldn't keep it from me but I also knew the feelings I was having. There have always been an unexplained connection between Annie and I. She was having a baby, our baby, with another man. Whatever her reasons, I looked down at my own son hours old laying in his moses basket peacefully, things were complicated before but I couldn't complicated them with children involved, *could I*? I set out to ask the question once and for all.

DEAREST ANNIE (*I typed*)
I CANNOT STOP THINKING ABOUT THIS. I THINK I KNOW THE ANSWER, I THINK YOU ARE GROWING OUR CHILD IN YOUR BEAUTIFUL BODY. I KNEW THAT WHAT HAPPENED IN LONDON WAS SPECIAL. WE'VE ALWAYS HAD A CONNECTION, FROM OUR FIRST MEETING WE'VE BEEN PULLED BACK TOGETHER EVERY COUPLE OF YEARS. NOW WE HAVE A BOND. A BOND THAT IS BIGGER THAN ANY REASON NOT TO BE TOGETHER.
ANNIE I LOVE YOU WITH EVERY BONE IN MY BODY.
SOMETHING MADE ME CONTACT YOU AGAIN TODAY.
BE MINE ANNIE? *Send*

I fell asleep waiting for a reply, perhaps even dreaming of a knock at the door and opening it to find her standing there, babe in arms. But it never came. Finally I sent my last ever email to her.

THIS WOULD HAVE BEEN AMAZING. GOODBYE ANNIE X *send*

The first 2 weeks were the hardest of my life. I was grieving for Lizzy, longing for Annie and juggling a newborn baby. Without him to look after I think I would have gone under but his survival depended on me. We slept in the same bed, scared he would leave me to. I spent hours telling him about memories I shared with his mum and Annie but mostly and probably inappropriately about the sibling Annie was carrying.

I had relief and sleep for myself when others visited, choosing only to have a couple of hours to make sure I wasn't missed or missed anything with him, he was my universe. He even attended his mummy's funeral. He was silent throughout and though most people gave him sad looks rather than new baby cooing ones we got through it together. He was my son and I his father and that's all we needed.

It was weeks after his birth I awoke in a hot sweat, tears falling down my cheeks and the feeling like my heart had shattered. I dreamt Annie had died. I saw her laying in a pool of blood. Then floating upwards and blowing me a kiss. She was crying and sad, I followed her gaze and saw a baby dressed in pink laying in a crib. She was the spitting image of Annie but she had my lips firmly pouting and twitching in sleep.

This feeling of achy pain didn't leave me all day. It was evening time and still I felt sad. It felt real. The tears that fell were because my heart ached. Ached at a dream?

Knock knock knock

Seeing Andy standing on my doorstep took my breath away. I was nervous and self-conscious but mostly scared that this meant the feelings I had been experiencing were true. I offered him a handshake and greeted him by name which obviously took him by surprise.

Then I noticed her, laying quiet and still in her car seat. Was Andy really delivering me my *daughter*? I picked her out of her seat, Andy said nothing. I might not have even known he was there as I picked her up that sparkle re-appeared in me. This little girl was to change my world. I had a son laying asleep in his nursery, a room he would now share with his sister. I studied her, compared them, there wasn't much size difference. I was cooing at her, taking in her every pore, she was a mini Annie and there was no doubt she was also mine. She knew it too as she had sunk into the crook of my arm and nestled back to sleep. Selfishly I hadn't seen Andy walk towards the door, I only looked up when I heard the catch click open.

"And Annie?" the words came out before I thought about them. I saw hurt in Andy's eyes. I didn't really expect Annie to jump out of her husbands car to stay with us but I needed to know if this horrid gurgling in the pit of my stomach was true, *though I long to be wrong.*

"It was her final wishes for her daughter to be with her true father."

Ouch, no, No, NO.

The air sped out of my lungs and I couldn't refill them fast enough again. My legs wobbled in confusion but I held it together. I was holding the closest thing to her but my love for this pink bundle would never take my lifetime yearning for her mother. I questioned what I knew now to be true.

"She's really gone?"

I ran through my dream, I knew she'd gone the moment I woke up this morning but my heart wouldn't let it in. How was I never going to hold her again, smell her neck? See her tease me and chase after her. How was I never going to make love to her to her again? We had had many goodbyes in our history but never this permanent, there had always been another meet place or stolen text, email. Ours were more 'see ya soon' than goodbye.

I caught the back of the door as Andy left, maybe survival mode kicked in but I didn't know anything about this baby in my arms. The 'nature and nurture' I could deal with but could it be that I had to ask another man my daughters birthday and even her name. *Surely there was only one name she could have?*

I met Andy's eyes, "Her names Bella - Annabel," *perfect* "and her birthday is February 29th." and he was gone.

I was left gob smacked. I had to deal with this burning grief building up inside. Annie had gone but in doing so she had given me Bella. I wanted to cry but my shaky feet took me upstairs and into the nursery.

As I lay them side by side they looked identical. I had two children, babies. Both with no mother, both sporting my pouting plump lips and both born on February 29th.

I couldn't believe it. The tears ran from my eyes. I'm not sad they are tears of joy and yet confusion. Two babies to grow together. Brother and sister, my son and daughter, my Bella and Jacob.

SEVEN

I was surprised how fast sleep came. I had left the babies together, they were sleeping soundly in identical positions on their backs with their arms in the air like they were being held at gunpoint! It had taken me a while to pull myself away from them but my bed called and so did Annie's memory. I wanted to snuggle up in my bed and think back over our times, 'us'.

The tears fell silently, easily and uncontrollably. I wasn't sobbing in grief just happily remembering but the thought of Annie and I never making any new memories was unbearable.

I only had two photos of Annie, the two I had received on her email. I decided I would make a box for Bella of all my 'Annie things', emails, photos. I would start with the postcard from Ibiza she had sent me before we realised I was on the same holiday. It quoted 'Wish You Were Here!' and I received it when I got home after spending a week with her on the beach on the front of the card! I also had a vial of sand from that beach that had become 'ours'. The CD of 'Finally Found' would lay on top, its words more poignant now than ever.

I awoke after dreaming about her. The kind of dream that makes you not want to wake up, pull the duvet over and spend time remembering its contents but the kind you can never get back into. The kind of dream you can actually feel in your heart, the warmth, the smiles and in my case the love. I'm sure I must have been smiling all night but increasing muttering from the nursery brought me back to reality, a reality without my dreams star. As I walked into the nursery the sun shone brightly through the blind housing an embrodied star making a shadow on the opposite wall. I looked around, I'd have to double everything I had, but thanked that I had anything to begin with.

I looked down. Their presence made me breath in sharply. They were both awake, the sharp intake of breath was for the staring, staring up at me with my eyes. They had obviously been discovering each other as they had little scratch marks on their noses and cheeks from their fingernails I had yet dare to cut. Still to young to move or roll they lay as I had put them. I smiled at the thought of me trying to feed them both simultaneously. This, along with everything else, would be a challenge from here on in.

I scooped them up using both my arms out in front, this would work so long as they didn't grow longer than my forearm anytime soon. I headed downstairs and placed one of them on the bouncer and the other on one of the big floor beany cushions. My dark oak laminate floor didn't seem such a good purchase as it did before parenthood. Once crawling came it would be a slippery journey! I grabbed two bottles from the kitchen and naughtily zapped them in the microwave. I didn't know how much Bella drank. I didn't know anything about her but as they lay along my thighs draining the formula I knew I had all the time in the world to find out.

They slept again and I began to appreciate this great thing about them being newborns and they would sleep a lot when I needed to get things done.

This morning I loaded onto my laptop a picture of them sleeping side by side on the floor cushion in front of me and made it my desktop wallpaper. *huh 'the twins"* I thought. I loaded the Kiddicare website and purchased the 'pink' equivalents of what I already had in blue. She would need clothes too as this morning she was in the last of the clean baby grows she arrived in and had one of Jacobs blue vests underneath.

Now I decided, it was time to ring mum, *deep breaths.*

It wasn't the type of conversation you expect to have but I didn't want them turning up and just seeing her. Besides I was hoping Mum would buy her some clothes on the way over as I certainly wasn't ready to leave the house with them both.

Until my order arrived I had a single pushchair and one car seat. The conversation was the stuff of Jeremy Kyle, 'Mum here's the grandchild no one knew about, including me'. It took me back to the day I told her about Jacobs pending and realised that was tarnished with an Annie memory just like today's conversation had been.

Seeing Mum hold Bella now though I knew we would all never remember a time she wasn't part of the family. Mum cuddled her tight smelling her head occasionally. Dad sat next to her holding Jacob. They kept looking from one to the other like they were playing 'Spot the Difference' with my offspring. There were no differences, both their mummy's had had little input into their physical appearance it seemed.

"It's amazing." said mum through tears of happiness, I hoped.

"They're identical, really identical. Huh, things like this just don't happen do they." questioned dad, the situation not getting into his understanding.

"You haven't heard the half of it," I said quoting one of dads clichés. "They were both born on the same day too!" I watched their mouths fall and then curl at the edges with the events surprises. Mum mockingly slapped her forehead with her hand and they both shook their heads.

"Who'd have thought it, 'twins', 'twins' for my little boy!"

My eyes hung as she said it. She picked up on my mood change and handed dad both babies complaining at the logistics if he had an itch but one gurgle from them and he was back to starring at them whilst they scanned their new guest.

"Oh son," She held me tight. "How will you do it? We are here you know, whenever you need us. We can help, we want to help."

"Its not that mum." I snivelled like a school boy with a cut knee into mums shoulder. She was smaller than me so the tears fell vertically to the floor rather than down my cheeks. "She's gone mum. How can I never see her again? I need her. They need her." I pointed towards the 'twins' who were starting to wriggle much to the horror of dad who struggled to contain both.

The routine of bottle making broke me out of my grief tears. I handed the warm bottles to my parents and closed my eyes, just for 10 minutes.

The days began to fall away into routines of nappies, bottles, napping and remembering. I spent every night starring at the stars once the 'twins' had gone to bed. They were getting so big and as their faces began to house smiles and a cheekiness that I knew came from me I began looking towards our future and less of looking back moping. More often than not I'd stay star spotting until my eyes rolled and I fell asleep. Thinking about Annie ensured I'd dream about her, alive and well, and with me. It gave a whole new meaning to the phrase 'living in a dream world'.

The decision to move away wasn't one I thought over for long. As soon as I heard of my Grans death and the auction of her large white wooden clad, beautiful double fronted house in Canada, I knew it was the place I wanted the kids to grow up. It was hard to explain to the ears I told. They thought I was mad, running away and maybe I was but if these past few weeks had showed me anything it was to believe that Everything Happens For A Reason and this opportunity was screaming at me as a reason not to be missed. I had many fond holiday memories there. My Gran was the cool grand parent who we were never allowed to talk about due to her running away, divorcing my granddad who had become a big part of my dads life when she left. Her house seemed a safe place full of new opportunities and with every trip here reminding me of places I went with Annie, new opportunities in a new country was perfect.

Telling mum was emotionally hard. Telling dad was harder due to the stories his dad had told him about his mum and now not only was I was going to live in a different country to them but it would be in her house! I truly expected them both to come too but instead it all past by quickly. They threw me a party, helped me pack and never mentioned tagging along. I wasn't sure how I would cope on my own as they had become regular visitors since the 'twins' arrival but before I knew it the day had come.

There were just two things I had to ask mum to finish off for me as I tied both the kids in the back of the car, a newly brought Chrysler I had had shipped over before our departure. It had replaced my old vehicle that I didn't trust to get to Asda let alone following our haulage to Canada!

Our car was packed with everything we might need for the first week as I'm sure we'd arrive before the truck. It included what seemed like hundreds of nappies, a fair few sterilised bottles, at six a day times two kids equals a lot of formula to house.

Mum took my two favours, the two envelops. One contained £4,000 that I was sending to the hospital I guessed Annie was in when she died. It was their local hospital and I figured they could use it to buy some new machine or do something up in the name of Annie and she would be remembered every time someone read her plaque. I wrote Annie Harper - *damn* - Annie ~~Harper~~ Turner Memorial.

The second envelop was a polite note to Andy. I didn't know if I owed him anything but he had had the courage to deliver Bella to me and for that I would forever be indebted.

Seeing mum and dad waving in the rear view mirror put my decision to the test. I broke a few times to turn around and pack them in the boot too but they had never seemed like they wanted to come as I had planned. They had a life here, friends, home and all I had here was them. I headed onwards to the ferry port to battle a weeks stay onboard until our new homeland shone on the horizon.

Pulling up outside the big white building was bewildering. This was the house my kids were going to grow up in. I had won the auction before it had gone to public, a clause I was very pleased Gran had added, wanting it to be kept in the family. It had cost me a fortune. Lizzy's life insurance had paid out to cover the mortgage on our old home which had meant its sale had given me a large lump sum and with a loan from mum and dad I had afforded this, a dream home.

Opening the front door with two car seats at my feet I stepped onto the soft and deep woollen floors I had chosen back at home out of a catalogue. It was echoy with no furniture to bounce the sounds from but full of light. The ceiling high sash windows threw shafts of sunlight across the floors. From the few steps of a hallway I could see the whole downstairs. To the left was a snug, a large open fireplace separating it from the rest of the open plan ground floor. The kitchen, in cherry veneer, was very up to date for a women who lived on delivered micro meals in the end.

I looked up and the front windows continued to shine onto a galleried landing housing all the bedroom doors off it. The house had been sprayed white all over at my request and Gran had given the furniture to the local charity bus in her will. In short it was beautiful ready to go family home so I lifted my family in to start living.

FOUR YEARS LATER

Looking up at the stars, delivering my nightly speech to Annie...

'They tried their uniforms on today. It was unbelievable Annie, they are just too small to be starting school tomorrow. They're still my babies.'

I smiled remembering having to pull Bella's tights nearly up to her armpits so her toes were in the ends.

'I never imagined if we'd have a child that I'd be doing all this alone. You should be here tomorrow, and everyday. We stood be standing together at that gate watching them go'.

I had long since forgotten that Jacob wasn't Annie's. When Bella spoke about her mum, Jacob did too. I didn't correct him, probably selfishly. They are known as 'The Twins at number 42' so for ease it stuck. I would tell him one day when he was older but I feared he would feel rejected. When we moved here none of Lizzy's family batted an eyelid. They visited him only once after her death and I had had nothing since. It became the norm to tell Annie about them both, I knew she would want him.

He was such a cheeky chap. Always laughing and I doubted the 'Kids laugh 300 times a day' theory with him. They were great together. They played happy and though there was squabbles they enabled me to work from home and be a full time single parent. All this would change of course once they were at school tomorrow as I had my first day in the office at a large law firm in town. It had taken a little more studying to change my British views to Canadian law enforcement but I had made it. Tomorrow we were all in for a change.

Their squeals filled the landing as I continued to talk to Annie on her star. Their toys, voices and chocolate treats had filled this now well lived in house. We were established in the neighbourhood. The kids would happily play outside with the other kids on our driveway whilst their mothers tried to fix me up with friends or sisters. 'The poor single dad of number 42' they said but truth be told I was happy. The scene looked like something out of Stepford Wives all idyllic lawned gardens and neighbours chatting. Perhaps it was unbelievable that I could be happy but I was and I wasn't ready to let anyone in where Annie had last been, physically or emotionally.

Morning came and I watched them hand in hand walk through the gates of their new school to the class with all the other young first timers. All the other mums and dads sad and amazed this day had come so fast. They're lunch boxes bashed their legs as they spotted a familiar face and ran. Then Mrs Hardy rang the bell and they marched in penguin like to start their first day. I looked at their bright white shirts and hole-less trouser knees, would they ever look so new again I questioned?

The parents trailed off and I looked up at the sky. One cloud remained, I smiled. She had seen them.

EIGHT

I try not to think about what I lost. I spent many months grieving for my daughter. It was all I had in me to board that plane four years ago. I left the hospital with nothing. The mind set of Andy when he left me that note in hospital must have been bitter as he left me no route to even find my daughters grave. Bella had not even been registered when she died so it was near impossible to find her in death. The hurt stayed with me everyday. I understood his anger, I had in affect stolen away his child that night by revealing her true paternity so his revenge was to never let me to say goodbye to her too. I sent myself mad searching for her and him from my hospital bed but one day I had to realise I was wasting the life I still have, and the life I fought for, and I took the step to leave England.

I hadn't known my destination until I reached the airport. Whichever flight left first was my frame of reference. I had no baggage, I had nothing.

The taxi had drove past my old home at my

request on the way to the airport. I had sent many letters from hospital, the kind nurses posting them for me on their way home. But eventually they were returned to sender by the new inhabitant.

There were 2 strangers cars parked outside on the driveway. New curtains at the windows and new plants starting to grow in the door side beds. I had tried to figure out how he had done it. How he had cut me out so easily, so quickly. Where had everything gone. Where had my car, clothes, belongings gone?

That was my feeling in the first weeks but now as I told the driver to drive on I didn't care. He could have the lot.

My only requirement in my destination was that it had to be an English speaking country so I could start work quickly. I only had the anonymous £4,000 that was left by my bedside. The nurses were unable to tell me its benefactor. It had come in special delivery for 'Annie Turner Memorial', thankfully when I survived it had been handed to me. The nurses all wanted to believe that it was from my husband and that he was apologising but there was not enough money in the world for what I had lost and I knew it could have only have been from one man. The envelop read Annie ~~Harper~~ Turner. It was him, my Eskimo.

Harder than leaving the country my child was buried in was leaving the country my Eskimo still resided. After all Bella no longer needed me and was at peace but he was still there. I could never face him again. I ached when I thought about keeping Bella from him. How could I have even thought it. If I had gave into my feelings I had in London, never left then we would have learnt of Bella's pending and would have been a family unit to this day. I took his child and his heart away and I can never forgive myself. I knew from the envelop that he had been told I had died, probably by Andy wanting the satisfaction, and I decided that probably was for the best. He could grieve for me and move on. I had caused him enough heartache, if I truly loved him I had to let him be happy. The 'What Ifs' could send a person insane and the day I gave up Bella's ghost I too gave him up.

It was with a fresh face and outlook I stepped off the plane. Those first few weeks were hard. I found an apartment and now appreciated why when they said it was a steal because it had no heating they were feeding me a line. Knowing I was new to the country and had no idea how bloody cold it got here in the winter. But it became home. It wasn't in the nicest part of the lovely town of Spruce Grove in Edmonton, but it was close to amenities and with every spare penny spent adding a little more homeliness to it the better it got. It was a one bedroom with open plan kitchen separated by the only bit of furniture included, a wooden dining table, from the lounge. The bedroom was down a short hallway along with the bathroom.

It was in need of a lick of paint, but slowly Marmot Avenue, Flat 6B was a nice place to be. I enjoyed making it like a shiny new penny but most of all, My shiny new penny.

Having spent all my money on the apartment and heating I needed a job and spent my days delivering sandwiches and my nights cooking at the lodges in the snowy districts. There was always someone in the lodges and if you could afford one of them, you could afford a cook to go with them. It kept me well. I didn't have anytime to spend the money I was making so my savings gathered speed and by my sixth month here I had enough to put down a mortgage deposit and buy the apartment I had made home. I didn't have time to miss my roots nor crave the life I had left but they still visited me every night during sleep. I would wake from a dream where we were all together and the feelings of being lost and alone hurt the most then. Then the work would start and I would visit the office blocks where bosses got to have photos of their families on their desks and I didn't even get a raised head when I walked in. Yes it was lonely but maybe I needed that time to make myself strong again.

The following months the resorts got busy and I was able to quit delivering sandwiches and work full time at the lodges. This found me new friends in the students that arrived from various college breaks and though I think at 34 they saw me as more of the sensible carer, I still had people who knew my name and asked me how I was. It was all their talk about college that took me back to when I went to school. Growing up I loved school. I was one of those kids who was academically good at everything and always, *always* wanted to be a teacher. I guessed at my time in life, though I didn't feel old, I was too old to be thinking about a new career. Whether it was the new me or just because I had nothing to loose I applied to become a Teaching Assistant at the school in Spruce Grove town.

It took awhile for me to hear. During which time I became depressed again. Wondering how I could let myself think I had a chance at starting again, doing something I had wanted in my old life. Then seven months later, the end of spring term they inviting me for an interview. It came with mixed feelings. Gratitude that finally someone saw something in me that was worth a meeting. Confidence that I had felt able to move on and sheer terror. Not one point had I considered returning to Time Publications after all the mess but now they required references from them at interview. With trepidation I made the call. I decided I would call for HR and there for didn't think I would have to say who I was or what it was regarding, HR get all kinds of crap calls all day long. As the ringing started I prayed Jenny didn't answer the phone. She did. She told me, or rather the lady I pretended to be that there no longer was a HR department and that all reference calls go to a direct department, *shit*.

Quickly thinking I decided I could pretend to be calling asking for a reference for myself as someone else. My dodgy accent got me through to my old supervisor and before I knew it the fax was being sent. Unbelievable, things appeared to be going my way. Three weeks later and I got the job and that about brings me up to date. Four years after waking up in that hospital I now sit in the classroom that tomorrow, the first day of school, will be full of first time 4 year olds.

In their starch white uniforms and the creases still on their shirts the 26 pupils lined up in front of the classroom door at 9am sharp. They were so tiny, all excited holding their lunchboxes and book bags. It was a new start for me and a new start for them.

Sitting for the register for the first time I saw all the backs of their heads starring towards Mrs Hardy. Everything a new experience. I was given a group of 7 to snail around the school halls with. Showing them where they play, queue for lunch and where their mummies will be waiting later. I got to know my 7 well and learnt not to take the '2 point 4 family' as 'normal' when kids were having grandparents and mummy's boyfriend pick them up! One boy delighted in 'beating' the other kids by having two mummies!

Sitting down for lunch with the other assistants,

it seems there is fine line between assistants and teachers and it is different tables at lunch! We all had good stories from our groups youngsters innocence and sadly one women told us that she was surprised that girls bitching started way before your teens. She had intercepted a group of girls not letting another play because her denim jacket had stars and theirs had hearts. A few of the kids we had found out had called us mummy when their conscious had forgotten they were no longer at home. After lunch we had a story and their ages really hit me as some of them drifted off during 'One Upon a Time'. I gazed out of the window. I had been so happy here today, so ready to experience my new future that I had yet to think of my past. It was the first time it had took them so long to enter my thoughts almost home time, 3pm and their first thoughts were coming to me. I always remembered Bella's home coming first. Though it had been the beginning of the end, seeing her in her nursery, tucked up asleep before I went in for my hug. And the memories of my lover changed as I re-called our past. Normally whatever I was doing I had memory of him that I could relate.

To say I was snapped out of my walk down memory lane was an understatement. I hadn't really calculated that Bella also would have been starting school today. Strange how I had started school on what would have been her first day. Without realising I was picturing her in her uniform, I put her in uniform of the school I worked at, I didn't know any others. Hair in a ponytail as I would have let it grow long like mine. I couldn't picture her face, how she would look now but those navy eyes she shared with her father would be deep and understanding. I had no doubt she would have been like a sponge at school should she have lived to attend. Hers lips would be prominent but would only become her attraction once she realised the world of boys and painted them with lip gloss.

I turned my head and it was a second before I realised I was no longer daydreaming. The vision of Bella stood in front of me. Hair still as mine, high in a pony like I'd put her in not five seconds ago. Her eyes were looking back at me, it was like I was falling into her fathers all those years ago.

"Where do I go for my coat Miss Harper?" she asked me in the first English accent I had heard in years. Her talking was the only way I knew she wasn't still the figure in my imagination. She was amazingly beautiful, like I thought moments earlier her eyes were like pools of the ocean, so deeply set into her face. Her lips could have been ripped off her father and planted onto her, she still had my hair. She was taller than a few of the other kids and was confident to have approached me, a stranger. My silence made her follow the crowds of other 4 year olds to the cloakroom and out to their families.

She had walked away and I couldn't move. It was her, I felt it, I knew it, but how ridiculous, it cant be her. My Bella died. I was in a country far from 'home'. Maybe working with children after everything I had been through was a step too far, especially today.

She was walking out of sight now and lost her in the other kids. Panicked I jogged towards the corridor between the classroom and the cloakroom. I found her reaching up pulling her jacket off her peg, a denim jacket, thankfully with hearts. She struggled with the arms but with help from her group leader she wondered out towards the proud mummy's and daddy's waiting for their 'grown up' children after their first day at school. I waited until the room emptied slightly before locating the name tag above the peg I saw her at. With a lump in my throat I pulled the PE bag to the side revealing the name.

BELLA

My heart jumped and ached and my legs wobbled. This wasn't possible. It was her in features and her by name but it couldn't be. Surely this wasn't real. Surely I was dreaming or still staring out the classroom window as five minutes previous. I was scared that she was real and scared that she wasn't but what scared me more was the fact she had walked out of the cloakroom and I had no idea where she'd gone.

The light flickered in my eyes and I jumped to the window. The door was crammed of little ones crying not wanting to leave or running too fast to their loved ones, bottle necking the exit.

My eyes searched the crowds but I didn't have to for long. I saw her running, laughing and shouting.

"Daddy!"

He stood out like a sore thumb. Picking Bella up and swinging her around. He was smiling and she was laughing. It was like something out of an advert, but it was real life, *wasn't it?*

I couldn't take my eyes off of them. I stumbled and my bum found the window ledge. My view was hindered but I couldn't stand and see this so-called reality. The thoughts racing around my head. The Whys and How's. What the hell was going on? I stood up too look again and he looked straight back at me. There must have been a good 70 meters between us but he held my gaze. He had the same bewildered look on his face as I did. He put down another child, a boy, perhaps one of Bella's friends had insisted on a swing too? His luscious lips parted to speak but our gaze was lost by a cold hand pulling at my arm and yanked me with force backwards into the book cupboard. The view from my happy past replaced with darkness and pain at the hand around arm. *What the hell was happening now?*

I met a pair of eyes in the darkness, another pair of eyes I knew, another pair from the past.

NINE

Andy was wired. He was as angry as I imagined the Andy who had left me for dead the evening I fell down the stairs. My mind was now a complete mess, I was certain this wasn't real and certain I would need specialist care at this rate if it was.

He was hushed but angry. The blood pumping through him so fast his face was red, his eyes so wide I could see the whites all around them. I was in complete shock. I couldn't understand how any of this was happening yet the pain I was feeling was real. Pain in my heart at the vision outside and pain around my arm as he squeezed it and rammed his hand over my mouth.

The children may have left but the staff would still be around and for who knows how long. This would certainly cost me my job as I am found in the book cupboard alone, scared and talking about people who were an ocean away but I needed help. I kicked the bottom of the door and a stack of books fell to the floor. I kicked again but felt a sharp scratch on my neck. The darkness fazed and the lightning flickers appeared. I felt heavy and sleepy, without being able to fight it I slipped to the floor. Alone with a man who had left me for dead and a mind full of confusion.

TEN

Lugging Annie out of the cupboard past dark was a difficult job. She was heavy under the sedative and her limbs were falling all over. It was doubled in difficulty as I knew a caretaker lived on the campus and would no doubt notice a man carrying a women out of a locked school at nearly midnight.

I put her into the back seat of the car, it reminded me of when she was doubled in pain and I took her to hospital only to find out she was pregnant, back when life was normal and we had a future to build. I tried to remain angry as this picture of happiness filled my mind. This women had ruined my life and continued to do so from the other side of an ocean.

I had learnt of her whereabouts when she had requested a reference for a new post at the school I had just carried her out of. It normally wouldn't have bothered me, I would have been pleased that she was going to permanently be away but when I heard the location it made me furious. I couldn't believe they again could have found each other by 'mistake'.

I had known of Bella's new life with her father and brother in Canada since before her first birthday. Her father had sent a note to me thanking me for giving him Bella and continued to tell me that everywhere he went reminded him of Annie so he had moved with his 2 kids so start afresh in Canada. The way he thrust his happiness into my present again had sent my blood to boiling point. I had broke my hand when Jenny suggested I 'get over it'. He had already cost me Annie, Bella and now Jenny was leaving ducking my fist and causing the broken bones on the wall behind her wasn't a good continuation point for this relationship, of sorts, to last.

I had been watching Annie for days. She certainly didn't know of their existence given the apartment she lived in and the sad expression she wore. How did this keep bloody happening? There was no such thing as a 'connection' between people yet my wife and this man, no matter what, had landed in the same country, same town and she was about to come face to face with her dead daughter at her first day at school.

Annie's head hit the side of the car as I drove too fast through the streets thinking of all of the above. It had angered me again and thankfully put me in the mood I needed to be in to finally stop this for good.

The bang against the door had aroused Annie and she was looking at me confused. I guessed she was somewhere between sleep and awake. She couldn't form sentences and was getting angry at herself as her body wasn't responding to her requests.

I pondered whether a sedative should do that but who knows what I had brought and syringed into her neck. I had brought it on the Internet and though the World Wide Web is an incredible invention there were lots of faceless people out there selling Everything named as Anything.

I pulled up outside my motel. It was even worse than Annie's apartment and a far cry from the huge place my rival and his kids had brought across town. When I arrived here I sat outside there most afternoons. It was the first place I expected to see her, a happy family unit, united in anger towards me.

It appeared to be a busy time for him having two kids start school, they were in and out with bags of new uniforms and stationary. Whenever they left the house both kids were holding his hands and smiling, like some advert that was too good to be true. The kids were identical. There mustn't be much between them. I never saw a mother, a wife, a nanny and never Annie. This guy did everything himself and the mini-me's he was raising certainly appeared to be his world. I watched him, thinking he had my life. I had wanted him gone but given the situation there was a lot better way of dealing with this once and for all and cause much more pain this time.

Annie had manage to sit and was hugging her knees as I turned round to get her out of the car. She was shivering. I grabbed her arm and she tensed under the pressure. It was sore from where I had pulled her backwards into the cupboard. Thankfully she walked with me, folding her arms to keep out the cold and as self protection I assumed.

I held her close as I fumbled with the door and flung her towards the bed when it opened. The light was from some tacky lamp on a rickety table and the candlewick bedspread showed it didn't give much care towards its guests. It was perfect for the use I intended. To spill some beans. No-one stayed here for a romantic break or stop off, it was used by people in hiding or affairs or deals.

I locked the door and watched Annie. She wasn't trying to leave or fight she just sat there.

"I guess seeing your dead daughter has confused the scariness of this situation out of you," I smirked, I wanted her to scream at me, try to run. That would make me mad and I wanted to be mad at her. "Huh, how the hell have you managed it *again* eh?" I kicked her feet to get a reaction I required.

"What?" she blinked at my speech, "Managed what. I don't know what the hell you are doing. Did you expect a happy reunion? After all your seeing me back from the dead aren't you? As far as you know I died at the bottom of those stairs and you just left."

"Oh contre wifey, I have been watching you for a few days now, in that shit hole you live. Buying those 'make me feel better' chocolates and the amount of wine it takes you to forget every night its no wonder you buy that cheap plonk." she didn't look surprised, maybe all her 'surprise' has been used up today, "Pretty little thing isn't she?"

Maybe it was a step to far, Annie flew at me. Her blows to my arms and back stung but nothing like the pain she caused by taking Bella away from me. That's the pain I wanted her to feel and that's the pain I would give over the next couple of days. My plan was simple. We'd argue now, throw harsh words back and forth at each other, then I'd break down tell her I still love her and that deserves to be happy even if I cant. She'll run to him, I might even drive her. They'll have their reunion, happiness for one night then I'll take him. I wanted her to have heartache but I wanted him to have pain. She had given her heart to him and I was going to physically take his. Whether she witnessed it or not he was about to live his last 24hrs.

I pushed Annie away, she was still weak and I didn't want the energy she had left to be in beating me.

"How could you do this to me? Why did you take my daughter away from me, let me live these past 4 years thinking she had died, died in my arms as you watched me fall down those stairs. I have missed everything with her. She wont even know me. She is mine and you took her away." Annie cried

"Just like you did to me!" I yelled "I thought she was mine remember. Do you think delivering my daughter to her to her real father was easy. Seeing the man who had impregnated my wife. Seeing Bella nuzzle into him like she should with me."

"You didn't have to do that."

"Like I would keep her. A daily reminder of you and him. Looking into her eyes and seeing your betrayal, NO THANK YOU. I didn't want her and I don't want you!"

"How did you find him?"

"You weren't the only one playing away my love. Though it turns out my conquest was deranged and just happened to be the only person you trusted with your dirty emails."

"Jenny?" she gasped

"Oh yes wifey we were at it like rabbits. Dirty little thing she is. Not a weekday went by actually." I smarmed at her, "Well honey if a man ain't getting it at home, he's getting it somewhere." I winked, antagonising her.

"You bastard!" It was working. "You think it was about sex? I love him. I always have. You've got him to thank for being with me in the first place." She stood up face to face with me, she was now the one wanting to hurt, "The night I got drunk and agreed to go out with you was the night I got a text from him. He asked me if I loved him, all those years ago, I said yes. I've loved him from the moment I met him and then he told me he was back with his ex and that he had to be a good boy again. It was depression and rebound that pushed me towards you. Your whole warped world is because of him."

I slapped her hard across the face, whipping the cheekbone I used to kiss. Could this be true? Even those years ago he was around her. She was very drunk the night I braved talking to her. So drunk she hadn't even remembered our date the following evening. "You don't marry someone on the rebound. Our date might have been a jealously thing but you *married* me."

"I'd had enough of waiting for him, waiting for our stolen moments to become permanent. You were mature and once upon a time you seemed to dote on me. And love! I needed to be loved."

"I did love you." I sat down, "I still love you." *This was it, let the acting begin.*

"Still love me?" she screamed "How can you still love me you've pulled my heart out and watched me witness the impossible."

"Then go," I said "you don't want to be here, you never have it seems. Go to him and be happy. Live the life you should have had 10 years ago. Go!" She wasn't sure if I meant it, "GO!" I screamed and flung the car keys at her "His address is in the sat nav." she jumped up before I could change my mind. "And Annie," I called over my shoulder "be happy.".

With the cool breeze from the open front door on my neck I knew she had left. Things had gone to plan but I felt used. Had she really only chosen me because he was unavailable? Had he always penetrated our lives? I wasn't the one who was supposed to come out of this questioning, hurting all over again. I never thought where they met or when. I just saw them together once, creating Bella. I never saw the 'Love' comment coming and only knew about this bloody connection from the emails Jenny had punched me with. He would pay for this. I was ready to hurt him for the once he had taken Annie but loving her and stealing her, this was going to hurt him a lot more. And maybe, I angered, Annie needed to see it too.

A smile grew on my face. I would give them one night, one night to plan a future and then I'd arrive. I wasn't sure which implement to use upon arrival. It had to be fast as Annie would surely try to stop me if I strangled or beat him. I looked at the case I had packed on the dresser. This was America and I couldn't have packed a gun, knifes on the other hand were easy to buy I had found. The cold sharp blade lay under the towels. Reflecting everything around it. Reflecting my hurt. Reflecting my pain and it would reflect the blood slashed from his chest and the tears pumping from her eyes. Yes its reflection was paramount in the cause.

ELEVEN

Racing down the unfamiliar roads following the irritating voice of the sat-nav's queens English, the hire car was silent except for my ramblings. I was confused beyond belief and right now I didn't know what was true and what wasn't.

The last twelve hours had changed my life unrecognisably. It was the most information I could take. Bella was alive, bang. My lover was in this country, bang. They were together and I was driving to be with them, bang bang bang. Thoughts hurt my head, along with the lump I had from the car door. Andy was unbelievable. What did he get from stealing me for a few hours. He had hardly told me anything new. Maybe he had planned to but I had seen Bella first. If I hadn't have seen her with my own eyes I wouldn't have believed him anyway. And then seeing her running towards him, 'daddy' she had shouted and the pride on his face. He had caught my gaze but I don't think in a million years he thought it was me. For one he believed I was dead and for two he was in a new country. I think in an hour we may both believe we do indeed have a tie afterall.

What had made us both choose Canada? From what I can remember neither of us had any connection to it and for me it was simply far away enough to get away from my thoughts and the plane was leaving quickly after I arrived at the airport. I didn't think he knew I was here. There was no way, I was dead to him and he would have made himself know if there was any belief in him that I was around.

Oh god how was I going to explain letting him think I was dead. I wanted no more lies. I had done it for the best. I could only apologise. I didn't know how this was going to go. He would surely be in bed. Should I break and enter and surprise him, no. If that happened to me I think I'd died. But if I knocked the door would he hear it?

The sat-nav showed the chequered flag on screen to show my finish line. Whatever was going to happen it was going to happen soon. I pulled into Greenwood Drive. It was smart looking with fields behind all the houses. They were huge with spread lawns and double garages. Double fronted with pillars, how was he affording this? It was the loveliest part of Spruce Grove and the kind of place I dreamt about when I laid my head down at my flat. The women on the sat-nav spoke, 'You have reached your destination'. I half expected her to say 'Good Luck' but no. I turned the engine off and eyed the shiny '42' on the red polished font door. I hadn't pulled onto the drive, I didn't want him to look out the window and call the police or something. Likewise I didn't actually know if he would be welcoming me or wanting an explanation. After all I had left him in the lurch and maybe 2am wasn't the time for a reunion. All I knew was since seeing him my heart had skipped beats. I longed for him again, something I hadn't allowed myself to do in years.

I hadn't thought about the time to much. Yes I knew it was late as it was dark and cold but once Andy had said to me 'go', I went. Maybe it was anxiety that kept me sat in that seat, looking down and playing with the key fob but I couldn't move. I had been so elated to think of a happy future I hadn't thought about if he wasn't in it with me. I thought about his words on the emails;

A BOND THAT'S BIGGER THAN ANY REASON NOT TO BE TOGETHER
ANNIE I LOVE YOU WITH EVERY BONE IN MY BODY.
BE MINE X

Lastly he had wrote that this would have been amazing. I smiled at the thought and turned to open the door and start that amazing life but the door wouldn't open. I looked up and piercing navy eyes stared back at me.

TWELVE

Seeing her again was like a dream but there she was staring back at me and I *was* awake. I had seen the lights come up the road and known I had to greet the driver.

Seeing her at Bella's school earlier sent a shiver down my spine. Though I had thought about it all day I had thought she was a vision. A vision because I had been thinking about her again so much.

Some days were easier than others but with preparing the kids for school I had really began to feel Annie was missing out. I spoke to her about it before I went to bed. I looked to the stars and told her our little girl was starting school today. That she looked to tiny in her uniform to possibly be big enough to be going to school. I asked Annie to look after her and when I saw her standing in the window in her classroom I thought she had done just that.

Now looking at her through the glass of a car window she was not a vision. She was real.

She starred back. Neither of us moved. I

wasn't blinking the tears away that were forming, I wasn't pulling the door open, I wasn't doing anything. Annie was here in front of me and I couldn't move.

She hadn't changed. Her hair was still high in a ponytail, a bright blond that defied natural. She was still beautiful despite the quivering lip and tears running threw her blusher. She was still my Annie.

I squeezed the door handle and it opened. She jumped as the warning beep came on to say her lights were still on. It broke the silence and the tension. Now when she looked at me she was smiling and her eyes were sparkling.

"Hello you," she spoke, I cupped her face and rubbed her nose with mine.

"Oh!" I sighed, taking in her scent. "What took you so long?" I joked and she laughed.

I picked her up and swung her like I do with the kids. She smelt amazing and she *was* real.

That moment lasted a lifetime. Under the stars that only yesterday I was talking to her too and now she was in my arms. We had so many questions but right now I wanted to hug her and not let her go.

I didn't want to share her but making our way inside I knew what it felt like to feel someone you had once lost again so through the door I took her up the stairs and towards Bella's room. I placed my hand on the handle but she stopped me. She shook her head and tuned back.

"Not like this." she whispered seeing the brightly coloured name plaque.

She wondered back down the stairs. I touched her shoulder and she turned crying into me.

"So many things are running through my head. I cant think what I want to ask first. I look at you and I cant believe it. I never want to stop touching you and then I remember she's upstairs and I ached to hold her. But...but,"

"But?" I asked, she was scaring me now, this wasn't a happy reunion she was hurting.

"But she doesn't know me."

I took her hand and turned her around. On the table I showed her a shoebox. It was full of everything we had shared. Photos, train tickets, Bella's wrist band from hospital. The emails we had sent. Laying on the top was the picture she had sent on the day we last had contact. Andy had long since been cut out of the picture and she stood pregnant by a huge Scottish fireplace. Another of Annie, her face and shoulders only so as not to cut to sharp a memory that she was dressed in her wedding gown. There was a vial of sand from Ibiza's best beach and the blanket we had been rolling on when evicted from the park. She lifted it and a dog-eared, nursery made mothers day card dropped out. I kissed her neck as she sorted through. "She knows you Annie, she draws you pictures and I tell her stories all the time."

Something changed in her. Was it relief? She

relaxed into my hug and held the card close to her chest. "I thought about her everyday."

"She'll wake up Annie and know you, we talk about you all the time." I met her eyes.

I held her gaze and the sadness was gone. She placed the card back in the box and closed the lid. Turning to me she brushed her lips with her tongue, not sexily but in anticipation. Gently she leaned in. It had been four years since I last kissed her. I had dreamt how this would feel, taste. I swore if I ever held her again I would never let her go but her lips didn't touch mine, instead our foreheads rested together.

"I love you." she said, eyes closed and close.

And I kissed her. She had never told me these 3 little magic words. I loved her too so much it had hurt. I loved her with every ounce of my body. My life was incomplete without her. I had lived without her and it wasn't right. She was home, in my arms and kissing me more deeply and emotionally than ever.

I held her tight. This wasn't about sex it was about love and our kisses never turned into the ripping of clothes. I wanted her but I wanted to feel her close more. Together we lay talking for hours. My arm had gone dead hours ago with her head laying on it but having her near, kissing me occasionally and stroking my arm. It was heaven.

"What time will she be up?" she asked, I too was wondering how much longer we had to lay together before a new day of meetings started.

"They normally get up around seven but run

into each others room rather than mine. I can normally get another hour before one of them shouts they are hungry or cant reach something." Annie had sat up and was staring at me. "What's up?"

"They? Oh god, I didn't think, you've got a family. A new life."

I calmed her with a kiss whilst she was still panicking. "There is no-one else for me but you Annie. I meant the 'twins'."

"Three kids, you've got three kids. Bella and twins?"

"No, I have 2, I guess they aren't twins with different mums but born on the same day to the same father, I call them 'twins'." Using my fingers as apostrophes.

She was baffled, "What? Who was born on the same day?"

Oh god, in my relief for normality and excitement in having her home I had forget that Jacob had arrived before Bella but after Annie had disappeared from my life. "Asleep upstairs is Bella and her brother, Jacob."

"No, Jacob died. Bella was a twin but Jacob died, months into my pregnancy!"

Huh, what was going on? Now it was my turn to be confused.

"Annie, I have a son, Jacob, who was born on 29th February, same as Bella. They are identical. Bella was a twin?"

"Yes. I lost Jacob, my boy twin, *our* boy twin before I knew I was pregnant with Bella."

"Whoa.. this is all to much."

"I didn't think today could get anymore stranger but yet it has!"

With that she nuzzled back into me and I told her all about the kids growing up. I made reference to Lizzy and how she had died. She had cried when I told her about Bella being dropped off and me not knowing anything about her. I had her registered back in England along with Jacob. Both mothers deceased and the same father they quickly became known as the 'twins'. I told her about moving here because my Gran had this house when she died and it came soon after I learnt of her death. She told me the money I had sent to the hospital had enabled her to buy her plane ticket here and we quipped at the many times we must have been in the same place but never crossed. How she had chosen a brand new career at the school the kids would join on the same day she did. We dug through photos and both were sad that we had not one of the four of us. We decided this week would be the time for our first portrait.

Annie cried when she asked me to forgive her for letting me believe she had died. I told her how my heart had ached the morning I woke up after dreaming she was gone and then having it confirmed by Andy. I told her I could understand how seeing me would have made her crave Bella, who she believed had died and we drew a line under it. We had each other now and the hurt and pain seemed a million miles away when I held her close once again.

The light began to crawl through the curtains when I started making breakfast. I honestly didn't know how the kids would greet her. I half expected Bella to walk down the stairs and hug me morning as usual and wonder over to Annie and do the same. She would know it was her I was sure.

We had spent the evening chewing the past and arranging the future. At any moment our future would come running down the stairs after not finding me in my bed. I would take Annie up there tonight. Last night was for talking and closeness and tonight I would make love to her like I had wanted too every night since we'd met. It was hard to believe that during our lifetime together we had only been together three times, all in London and one had created our baby. Yes I had craved this women since her existence but having her, knowing her, spending time with her, loving her was as infectious as making love to her. She made me smile just by entering a room. Seeing her finding her way around my kitchen, juggling many different breakfast materials as she had no idea what the kids would eat. It was bliss. It was magic, it was our connection, it was simply 'us'.

I heard a bang from the back door. Thinking one of the little monsters had again thrown a wounded soldier out the window or Jacob had thrown

Bella's doll, I went to inspect. Nothing. Maybe the sunlight warmth was cracking the plastic on the conservatory roof. Maybe a stone from the road had flung up by a passing car. Maybe....

But it wasn't any of that. It was an intruder, an intruder Annie knew all too well running past me, towards her and branding a knife to her neck.

THIRTEEN

Grabbing Annie by the throat and seeing his face was worth the evenings wait outside. Picturing them getting cosy had riled me enough to burst in guns blazing, well knifes blazing anyway.

I had slipped the blade out of its protective towel at my motel. It felt huge in my grasp and I felt impregnated in its presence. I had made the right entrance, scared and panicked and it held the attention. His hand automatically shot in the air.

"OK Andy, lets stop, lets talk about this."

Talk? What was he a poof? "Oh yes, lets talk." I quipped levelling the knife to my side, mocking them. Annie went to move, believing my mock. I tugged her arm back and replaced the knife at her throat, this time slightly drawing blood. His eyes glazed.

"Oh right, you've only just got Princess Annie back, wouldn't want to loose her again, RIGHT IN FRONT OF YOU." I shouted.

Behind me I heard running footsteps on the stairs.

"Stay there kids." He put out his hands to keep them on the last step. Meters from me.

They both stared at me with his bloody navy eyes. I screamed throwing Annie forward and away from them. They followed her. Starring.

"That's my mummy!" Bella screamed and started to punch me in the leg.

"Mine too," the little boy started punching too.

Annie was starring, crying. Looking at them hitting me screaming, 'that's my mummy, that's my mummy'. She grabbed them both, scooping them both up under each arm like she was well practised. She ran past him and towards the safety of the back of the kitchen.

Like animals we paced round and round each other. Each waiting for the other to make the first move. I had the high road surely, branding a knife and reflecting his family huddled in the corner with every flicker of my wrist. What did this guy think he was doing. I knew one man protecting his kids is bigger than an army but in that kitchen I was the one on top. I was the one in the limelight and I was the one who would prevail.

I jerked occasionally to see him flinch. His eyes crossed back from mine, the knife and his precious cargo. Annie was holding them both tight, stroking their hair out of their faces, kissing their foreheads and whispering everything would be OK. They held onto her tightly too, screwing their eyes up whilst she said 'mummy's here, mummy's here'. The blood that oozed from the edge of the blade had dried on her neck. A little of her blood for drama and then a whole lot of blood for pain relief. My pain relief and his blood.

Then he launched at me. I hadn't expected it. I had been watching Annie, watching Bella. I had been the first to hold that girl after her birth and now her presence infuriated me. I had lost myself in her and his arms were around my chest, pulling the knife downwards and towards my thigh. He screamed to Annie get the kids outside. I was looking down, willing the knife upwards, into any part of him. Any part would make him stand back. I didn't want Annie to leave, I wanted her to see him crumble. This man she had put on a pedestal, to fall slowly in agony and out of her life.

Fuck! A sharp pain shot threw my knee as I realised the knife had inserted behind it. I stumbled and cried out. I grabbed him and we tumbled on the floor. Rolling over and over. My blood leaking onto the floor. We scuffled towards the door. Was he trying to get me into the daylight? All those people leaving for work all those witnesses ready to dial emergency services. I don't think so. He wasn't going to come out of this as a hero.

I stiffened and he found it hard to hang on. Finally I got my chance as he tried to re-grip me.

The blade disappeared easily into his thigh. I knew it would create a lot of blood, arteries run through there and what a painful way to die. The blood draining out of you and you helpless to stop it.

A change of plan and I threw him into the back of my car. He was limp and groaning. I was parked close to the front door and left the house behind easily. I had no idea where Annie was. Killing him and then taking his body was genius. She couldn't bury him, she couldn't see him 'one last time'. She couldn't get closure and that would surely break her heart like I had wanted into more pieces than I could imagine.

I sped off, him knocking and crying for help, his blood trickling threw the hire cars upholstery and the smile on my face growing and growing as his whimpers got quieter and I heard his last gasp.

FOURTEEN

I left the kids in the garage. It was the first time I had stepped out in the garden. I had yet to see the house in the light and finding a place to safely put the children was hard. I saw the tyre marks in front of the garage and hurried them in through a side door and locked them in the car. If we needed to leave quickly this was a good start. I put my finger through the keyring and ran back to the house.

I had never had so much to loose and holding that handle to the back door I had no idea what I would do but I had to help. I didn't know where a phone was to dial for police and my mobile was still in my bag in the car on the roadside from my arrival last night. I wasn't even sure I knew what to dial for help.

I slid through the back door and peered round the corner. The house was silent and I saw nothing, no-one. Happy that my path in front was clear I emerged deeper into the house. Where had Andy gone, what was he hoping to achieve?

Then I saw it. Splattered across the floor and

dragged towards the front door. Blood. Deep red blood. Whose? I had no idea. My heart quickened as I bent down to see it. There were footsteps in the congealed thicker pools. It made my heart race. The prints were of trainers and I knew Andy was the one wearing them. Did this mean he was dragging my man, dragging him leaving his blood behind? My hands cupped my mouth but not enough to stop the vomit from leaking out. I sobbed as I opened the front door. The footprints and tracks led to an empty spot, a spot I imagined not ten minutes ago housed Andy's car. The door frame held a perfect hand print, in blood vivid on the lacquered white wood frame.

I ran into the street. I saw faces but knew none of them. They looked at me strange for they knew me neither. I screamed for help and they flocked to me. I screamed for him to come back, for him to walk up the drive, for his hands to sweep me up off the floor I found myself on, my legs not able to take my weight and this burden. I screamed in pain as my heart skipped beats at the thought of loosing him all over again.

A neighbour asked about the kids, I was a stranger covered in blood and they were no where to be seen. I stood firmly and went to get them.

Sirens came along our street. What should have filled me with confidence only made me worse. What use were they now. Andy and him were gone. Maybe for good and maybe till he needed his next victim. He was set to shatter my life and shattered it he had, into a million pieces.

I sat on the sofa in the snug whilst neighbours rallied around with tea and breakfast for the kids. I didn't let them go. I held their free hand whilst they ate and hugged them close when they had finished.

Police tape had been erected over the front and back door. There were walkie-talkies crackling everywhere. Men in white suits with cotton buds were cleaning the floor whilst a lady officer tried to get me to talk.

"Annie is it?" she held out my handbag I left the rental.

"She's my mummy," Bella offered, making my heart jump. I had longed for her welcome but never like this. I stroked her hair and kissed Jacob's jammy cheek.

"I want him found." I managed, "I want them both found." Tears filled my eyes and the police lady placed a comforting hand on my shoulder.

It was evening and I felt nothing. The police were leaving. I was numb with their departure. They had nothing left to say or do. I was the one offering them the information, the little I had. I told them about the motel but was unable to help with the vehicle. I had taken Andy's rental from the motel to here so had he stolen another or hired one? I had nothing to say where he was or what he was doing. I didn't care. I wanted my

Eskimo back, in one piece, unhurt and beautiful as always.

By evening of the most surreal day of my life the 'twins' slept together in their dads bed. Soundly drifting off. I lay there too. I hadn't even entered this room before this evening. How was I supposed to lay in his bed, a bed that I had never slept in. Would I find comfort in his scent still being on the pillows, would it sooth me into sleep every night without him? I stayed awake. Convinced he would walk back through the door. He didn't. Would he ever? Who knows but forever I would wait, right here, with his children and longing for him.

I had rang his parents the following morning. It was an indescribable feeling. Sandra, his mother had answered and I had simply said 'its Annie' and she knew. I had never met her but she told me she knew all about me and my 'death'. Not just as Bella's mum but as she said 'her sons soulmate'. We both cried together. I could offer little condolence as I felt totally responsible for bringing it to her doorstep. I asked her if she could forgive me and she laughed.

"You gave my son life," she simply said, "for that I will forever be grateful. He worshipped the ground you walked on, whether it be the years you were apart or the days you were together, the smile on his face was because of you Annie."

It was hard to move past that. We were total strangers but tied together and with that her flight was booked and she arrived the following day.

TWO WEEKS LATER

The police had confirmed they would not consider placing him on the missing persons register because of the amount of blood, his blood, they had found in our home. Specialists had informed me they were treating it as murder and to start to grieve for he was certainly dead. With no evidence, information or leads the case was given a 'Cold Case' title and put on a shelf should anything come to light in the future with DNA. It was hardly comforting to picture DNA turning up 30 years away that proved he died by Andy's hand, Waking The Dead style.
There would never be a normal again but slowly we got into a routine. I had had help in telling the 'twins' about their daddy. I couldn't face telling them they wouldn't see him again. I thought it best they stick to being kids and being kids meant they returned to school the next week. I wouldn't return to my job. It was too soon. I had so much to learn and sort out. I had become a welcomed neighbour in the street and people were only to willing to tell their stores about my Eskimo. They had been my family since that morning, them and Sandra, who had continued to live with us much to the 'twins' pleasure. I needed all their comfort, especially today.

It was Sandra who suggested the goodbye. With no body we could not have a burial or funeral to attend. She suggested a memorial ceremony where we each place something into the ground of his. We could have a headstone and a place to go to think about him. So today we gathered around the hole in the wood Sandra had found since his bloody disappearance. Sandra's presence had been a godsend not just as she had arranged the entire day but at night when I lay my head on her shoulder and cried my heart out, the heart that belonged to her son.

Getting the 'twins' dressed that morning was hard. I wanted them to wear something their father would like but two four years olds weren't that helpful so they did what they wanted, something I worried they would get away with far to often from now on. I had dressed simply in a black dress and a colourful scarf. Underneath I wore one of his tee's. It didn't smell of him as it had come straight out his wardrobe but it had once been on his skin and close to his heart and that is what I yearned for.

The sun dappled down through the trees and shone on the plaque Sandra had ordered. My eyes were hidden by my sunglasses. The children had seen enough tears and though there was no chance of me making it through the day with them not falling at least I could hide them away from their innocent eyes. People were throwing their letters, prayers, memorabilia into the box and walking away. This was supposed to provide closure. A final goodbye and doorway to the future but I didn't want a future without him. People were trialling off. Finished with their goodbyes and I hadn't even started. Gatherers had looked at me to start to show them the way but I crumbled behind and Sandra took centre stage.

Now, as if she knew she bundled the kids back to the waiting cars. I perched hole side and saw the mounds of paper, CD's, newspaper clippings people had brought. I wanted to take the box home and have it there. More of him to keep hold of but I knew I couldn't. The 'twins' picture lay on top. It had made Sandra and I tearful when they first drew it. It was 'our' home, I hadn't got used to that yet. With five of us in the front garden. Them two playing, me looking bald as they had drawn my hair with a white crayon and Sandra looking unfortunately rounded. Stu, their Grandpa was merely a stick man as they had no idea what he looked like. In the blue sky was one cloud, on it lay their dad, looking down on us all.

I opened my cream parchment I had brought out of my pocket and began to read. I didn't know how far I would get but I wanted to read my goodbyes aloud, just me, and this dappled sunlight into a place I would come to remember him.

ESKIMO

HAD I EVER THOUGHT THIS DAY WOULD COME I WOULD HAVE HELD ONTO YOU THAT FIRST DAY WE MET ALL THOSE YEARS AGO. HOW AM I SUPPOSED TO MOVE ON, WE

HAVEN'T HAD THE LIFE TOGETHER WE CRAVE. WE HAVEN'T EXPERIENCED HALF OF WHAT WE SHOULD.

MY HEART ACHES EVERYDAY WHEN I WAKE UP AND FOR A FEW SECONDS I REMEMBER WHAT HAS HAPPENED. ITS LIKE I LOOSE YOU EVERYDAY.

I LOOK BACK OVER MY LIFE AND YOU PUNCTURE IT WITH MEMORIES, TOO MANY TO WRITE DOWN BUT THEY FILL MY MIND AND ONE DAY THEY WILL FILL YOUR CHILDREN'S TOO.

I CANNOT IMAGINE BRINGING THEM UP WITHOUT YOU. THEY LOOK LIKE YOU MORE AND MORE, THEIR SPARKLING NAVY EYES AND THEIR LIPS FULL.

THIS WASN'T THE WAY IT WAS SUPPOSED TO BE. PEOPLE SEARCH FOREVER TO HAVE WHAT WE HAD.

HOW CAN I SIGN OFF A LETTER I NEVER WANTED TO WRITE - I LOVE YOU JON, MORE THAN THEY WILL EVER INVENT A WORD FOR.

A XXX

I stood up, reading the plaque for the first time:

JON JACOB PARKER
LOVING SON
MISSED FOREVER

I took out the pen from my pocket and wrote:

JON JACOB PARKER
LOVING SON, **ESKIMO AND DADDY**
MISSED FOREVER
YOU WERE WHAT I LIVED FOR AND I WAS WHAT YOU DIED FOR

I placed my letter back into it envelop and threw it on top of the pile. I walked away and didn't, couldn't look back.

FIFTEEN

Driving, speeding away from Jon and Annie's house was exhilarating. I had done it, I had caused Annie the pain I wanted, I had taken him away once and for all. My only regret was I hadn't seen her face. I'd have liked to hear her screams and watch her face fall as his limp body had. With Jon's body coasting around in the back of the car I hadn't thought what I would do with it. Though I knew where I was driving too. I hadn't rented a room last night, I knew Annie would tell the police about my motel, good job I'd paid cash, and then I was too excited to sleep so I stole the car I'm driving and waited outside. I watched from the road, the lights in their house never go off, too much to talk about I had thought. I had pleased myself I had waited till I did. They could plan last night, let them dream and this morning I had took it all away.

I had been driving now for 3 days and the scenery was totally different. I had perhaps done 900 miles before I saw the sign I was looking for and crossed into higher, colder Canada for. I hadn't stopped for anything other than fuel or food. There was a poetic reference to my madness marathon.

As I started to see coast I crossed down an unused path just after a crossroad and saw some disused garages, perfect, no eyes and no witnesses. I could dump him and the car and it would be ages before they found him. Though if they did find him Annie would request his body and I couldn't have that, I'd have to bury him.

I pulled into one of the garages with no door. It was musty and damp in the back and looked like it had seen better days. There was barrels and rusty equipment that suggested this might have been a workshop, perhaps a mechanic, some years ago.

Where could I store him whilst I dug a hole, it would take some time. *How deep would I need to go?* This would be a hard job. The ground was covered in hard cracked mud and with only old tools it would be near impossible. I needed to go to town but Jon was starting to become an issue, driving a body around whilst shopping wasn't clever. Whilst driving here, day and nights I hadn't seen him laying there back there but now I had stopped I saw his face. The blood had dried around his leg and it was all the more real that I had committed murder. A sly grin raised on my face as I thought to store him in a barrel whilst I went to buy the things needed for his final resting place.

He was heavy and hard to hold. I had pulled him from the car, head first and dragged him across the floor of the garage. I had managed to park close enough to the garage floor so as not to discolour the ground with his blood. His head banged on the concrete.

No way, what was that sound, a moan!

As I wound the wire around his hands behind him on some rotten chair I found at the back of the darkness I wondered how the hell had this guy had survived. His head was low and he had little strength. There was blood on the back of his head but I couldn't work out if it was fresh or old. I was torn between happiness and panic. He wasn't in any mood to fight back which I was pleased about as maybe now I could see the light go out in his eyes first hand but panicked as I didn't know whether I could do it again. Before I had the anger of seeing Annie holding their love child and another, making a home and having the life I should have been having with her. But now I was stuck in the back of beyond alone and with nothing that would do the trick. I needed him to spar with me so I perked up and started to talk to him.

"Hey Jon, how's the leg?" he didn't move just twitched, perhaps he was slipping in and out of consciousness and my words had brought him round to confusion. I tried again. "No Annie to save you here Jon." His head lifted at her name. "Oh imagine her pain, seeing the blood on your carpets, alone with two kids, your two kids."

He spat blood, *yes* the head wound was new.

"Any idea where we are 'Eskimo'?" I got close to his ear, "Eskimo Point!" I sniggered. "How's the double irony. Her Eskimo resting forever at Eskimo Point, poetic beauty eh! There you were thinking she was dead for years and now you're the one to die. Did you like the time I gave you to remember, plan and celebrate Jon. Hey, no such celebrating for you now."

Eskimo Point had stood out like a neon sign from the map when I left Jon's in a hurry, like the welcoming into Las Vegas all lights and glitter. 'Eskimo Point' or Arviat, north east Canada, as it was known since June 1989 would be his finishing line.

He looked me in the eyes and tried to speak but couldn't. He was a mess. Perhaps I wouldn't need to kill him, perhaps he would *slowly* slip away, feeling the pain and knowing it was too happen. I could make it all the more painful though.

"I cheated on her you know. Poor Annie at home making a nest and there I was behind her back screwing away. We'd shag alright but she didn't want to, I'd roll on and she'd go rigid. I'd grind away on her Jon, your Annie, hours after fucking a descent lay and she'd just take it. Say Jon is it still rape if your married and she didn't put up a fight?"

Ouch! The pain surged through my face, my nose throbbing and dripping with blood. The picture in front of me hazy as the pain ran from my face into my temple, disorientating me. *Ouch. Holy fuck.* The bastard was fighting back!

SIXTEEN

Rocking along in the back of Andy's car was agony. I think we had been driving for longer than I was conscious for as the days and nights rolled into one and I lay still. I dreamt of my family at home. I had to get back to them. I had to get away from this crazed man and I had to get help. I was in pain and it wasn't getting better. I had managed to stem the blood flow from my thigh by pushing it against the seat cover. There was a leather strip between the seats thankfully as the fabric would have drank the flow and meant the end of me. I had to lay still. Having Andy thinking I was dead was the only way I could buy time. My body needed to clot the blood around my leg and I needed sleep to get strong.

The car stopped. All I could see was cloud and hear footsteps on the ground. The door clicked open, the cold came in. *I mustn't shudder.* Andy grabbed my shoulders and pulled, I crashed to the floor head first with a crack and it all went dark again.

My wrists hurt and I groaned at the new thunder in my head. Everything was too bright for my eyes and I heard Andy walking around me. I could see his mouth moving but then all I heard was mumbling, then clear as normal I heard him say 'Annie'. I looked up, opened my mouth but it was grinding pain to think. I spat the blood from inside my mouth. It was fresh. How could I do this with more injuries. I closed my eyes and saw them smiling at me, holding on to Annie's hand and running threw the grass together. Though they weren't running towards me they were running away from me. Further and further into the distance, I was loosing sight of them. NO, I wouldn't loose them. I summoned all the strength I had left to stand and spin the chair I was attached to round.

It smashed Andy in the face, and put him on his knees. Blood rushed from his nose and he cupped his face. After all he'd put me through and he was a wimp. I hit him again, the chair broke under its rotten pressure. With no chair holding them behind me I shook my hands free.

There is a difference I reasoned to a violent man and a man protecting his lot. The difference being I was going to hurt Andy until he didn't get up again to follow me, whereas I was being hurt for his pleasure. I jumped towards him pushing his head towards the floor. He screamed and I stood up. Looking at him he didn't even try to stand and in about five seconds I realised why. Reaching into his pocket he brought out the knife.

The heat raged through my foot as he left the blade in and dragged me into the boot of the car. The trunk came down on my head, he took the blade out, burning surged and the blood flowed. Again darkness drew from all sides until I was flat and I saw them running again. All three together hand in hand they ran through fields high with grass and tall daisies that caught Bella's hair and pulled it backwards as she ran. Jacob was grinning up at Annie, finally pleased to have a mummy to belong to. And Annie trotted along after them when they fell behind looking at a butterfly or a bug.

Then they all stood still and waved. The sun sunk behind them making my eyes swint. I blinked to see them clearer, they were gone.

SEVENTEEN

He fought a good fight I'll give him that but it had been his last. No sound came from the boot he was now laying in. Why hadn't I thought of the boot before, hidden away from prying eyes and mine. I was driving into town some 40 miles away, there was no way I was going to bury him now. I was making my way to the nearest petrol station, filling this car up and blowing it sky high. I could watch as the pieces came down and I could wonder which parts were Jon's and which were the moulting metal.

I filled up the engine and brought a jerry can and filled that too. I placed it on the back seat, parallel to where I reckoned Jon's head lay. I brought a pack of cigarettes and a lighter. I didn't smoke but a man buying both together caused less concern than I man buying a jerry can of petrol and just a lighter!

I had past the perfect location on the way over. A quiet road next to a cliff edge. If I was lucky the car would blow then fall down the hill and burn out before anyone could get there.

I day dreamed about the places I could go next. I had always wanted to visit Mexico and as it wasn't far, well closer than if I was back in England anyhow, I figured it could be my next call. What was the saying? As much tequila and ten dollar hookers you could manage, sounds like the perfect way back from murder and heartache.

I couldn't set my mind away from the sparing I had used on Jon. It had never been like that with Annie, had it? Was it rape if it was consensual but not really wanted? I had always loved the women throughout our marriage. Why else would I have gone to such lengths these past few days. I reasoned Love and Hate are very similar, the same part of the brain gets infected.

It was this thought that distracted me. Distracted me from the rigger lorry in front of me and the huge engine gauze coming my way. I twisted the steering wheel as far as it would go to the left, towards the hill, trees and...

The last feeling I would have would be about Annie. About how pain is a personal thing and getting revenge on her was not the route to my happiness. I thought about how she was hurting now, how Bella and her brother would be feeling, going through life explaining they didn't have a dad. About Jon, in the boot of my car, if not dead now then dead once we hit the hills floor. And I thought about me, the pain in my heart. It wasn't aching anymore it was stabbing, stabbing from the knife in my pocket I had used over these past days. Stabbing deeper and deeper, and lastly as it plunged through my lifeline and cut me off I gasped my favourite word. A word that had kept me going through all of this. My reasoning for everything, "ANNIE!".

EIGHTEEN

Andy's stolen car hit the oncoming rigger with force. The car spun round, it rebounded off the trees Andy had thought would take them down the hill but it cascaded back onto the road and sat there.

The driver got out of his truck, stretched and wondered over to the scene. The car had hardly made a dent in his front spoiler. Cautiously he got closer to the car, hands in his pockets, popping his head forward further but not his body. Not wanting to commit wholly but wait, he heard banging.

Slowly he moved closer to the car, wondering if he was risking his own life by opening the boot. He reasoned if it was a human in there surely he was in there for a reason. He got close enough to notice the jerry can on the back seat, this was some serious shit he had stumbled on. He tried the boot catch and to his welcome it clicked open.

The guy he found was a mess. There was a lot of blood all over him. It was impossible to see if he was still bleeding or it was old. His face was worn, tired and he wasn't talking but is outstretched arms meant he was still alive, barely. He couldn't let him walk away, perhaps he was a wanted man, it certainly appeared so by his circumstance. So he helped him out of the boot and moved him roadside. He lay back onto the grass and pebbles. His eyes rolled upwards and the truck driver felt sick.

He wondered back over to the car, to the front seat. Having seen Andy in the drivers seat, knife through his chest and definitely dead was enough to make him run. This wasn't what he needed to be associated with. It was an accident, his truck was not harmed and nor was he. He jumped back into his cabin and drove away. Certain another would be along shortly and be a braver man than he.

It was with reprieve he spotted the police car heading in the direction of the crash about 2 miles down the road. Was he doing his rounds or had he been called? If he was called didn't that mean there were witnesses? Who knew and who cared. He put his foot down and sped in the opposite direction fast. He had no desire to be the hero and he would be sure to see it on the news later.

The trucker pulled into a pit stop hours later. Tired from an eight hour drive, he put his feet up, removed his boots and clicked on the TV. His head heavy with thoughts about the man in the boot. He wondered if he was alive, if he was a wanted man. He was someone's son and he had left him alone, pulling him bleeding out of the boot of a dead mans car. He saw the scene again only this time it was on the TV and not in his head. He turned up the broadcast and listened.

...and finally tonight we head to our correspondent high in the hills to bring us an update of the bemusing tragic accident which occurred earlier today.

Resting his head on his hands, held up by his elbows, he was intrigued, *please let me have done the right thing*, he prayed.

Yes thank you Becky. I am here where not too long ago the wreckage of the blue car has been removed. We can reveal the car was infact registered as stolen some 3 days ago from a neighbourhood far south of here. Police inform us both men found in the car had no ID on them and they currently remain nameless.

We were told that the driver of the vehicle died on the scene. He had one severe knife wound straight through his heart. Paramedics say the impact of the crash had impaled him. Curiously the knife that killed him was in his own pocket. Forensics are saying that there appears to be dried blood on the blade and testing will be carried out to see if DNA can be gained and perhaps shed some light on the identities.

Bizarrely in another twist the man police found curbside was originally in the boot of the car as a trail of his blood followed back from there. We are told he has a number of injuries, old and new so he had lost a lot of blood. Witnesses at the scene say he was indistinguishable due to his injuries.

Not long after both bodies were removed from the wreckage police lost vital evidence as its thought there was petrol within the car that caught fire.

What happened here this morning appears to be an accident but knifes, a man in the boot and a stolen car, it seems this story is far from over. Becky, back to you.

None the wiser if his choice had been the right one the trucker moved on, knowing he would read about it in the coming days and then he and the county would forget all about it.

NINETEEN

TWO WEEKS PAST

Down in the forensic labs at the local police station, results were in, with a surprising twist. Not just the two victims DNA flashed up from the findings but another. It was easy to locate a body match for the second, it was from the man in the boot, but the third was older, drier blood. Female DNA, did this mean they were missing another body?

The DNA results flashed through the database. Since the tragedy of 9/11 forensic databases were worldwide catalogues so compared millions of people worldwide. This would take some time. The scanner left the computer searching and took a break.

Andrew Turner
Jon Parker
Annie Harper

The three names flashed on the screen when she returned from coffee. Printing their personnel details and walking them up to the incident room she flicked through the papers. The scanners eyes lit up as the identities became clear. A web of marriage vows, illegitimate children and emigration had come to light.

"This will be an interesting meeting!" she gleamed, "I've waited for something juicy like this for years." She entered the room, she wanted to be there when all this came to light.

"Right team, things have changed considerably with this new document. Gather round please, you're going to need to write this down its unbelievable. Firstly we have a name for the stab victim finally, Andrew Turner. Will someone get on to his next of kin, you. Probably in the UK as he, along with the others are all British. Er... yes next of kin details here. Thanks." he flicked through to the next page.

"Secondly the guy from the boot is er, Jon Parker. He emigrated here four years ago, he has two kids. Probable that his family still reside in England. That ones over to you. A father, London phone details, here you go.

And finally, ha-ha, scrap all of that, this is the deal breaker. The third blood belongs to a Annie Harper, who until recently went by the name of Annie Turner, victim number ones wife!" he turned to his colleague. "You cant make this up. OK maybe a crime of jealously? We should have this over by lunch. Someone get over to Mr Parker's house my guess is you'll find Miss Harper there with his kids."

Another officer, Jenkins stood, "Sir, I was over at this address two weeks back its not all black and white. We found blood everywhere. Sir we told her Jon was dead already!"

"Christ!" the constable grabbed his hat and offered the officer who spoke out a lift. There was only one way they were going to close this case and that was to find this Annie Harper and asked her what the hell was going on.

"Soft approach here I think Jenkins. Right now we don't know who has done what. We could be walking into a minefield of adultery and planned murder, people don't just end up in the boot of a car. I'll handle the questions, pretty women think they can get away with anything, even murder. Things don't look good for her Jenkins." he thought aloud "Her husbands dead and had a guy in the boot of his stolen car."

Had they planned it? Who had hired who? Who was with who and what is the link we were missing? He thought.

TWENTY

The day after the ceremony with the kids back at school after a very strange introductory and weepy conversation with their headmaster I went home to sort through the photos. It was a job I had put off until the day after Jon's memorial else I'd have put them all in the ground for him and had nothing for me. Getting to know my own child, children if Jacob had anything to do with it, through pictures I had never witnessed being taken was hard. I starred hard at each one. Seeing them develop from tiny newborns, to taking their first steps. There were Christmas costumes and Halloween outfits, each one cuter than the next. There wasn't an age where they didn't look like him. Sadly there were few of Jon. Being a single parent meant he was the one behind the camera and the only time they really were shown together was the leaving party in England before moving here when the 'twins' were young perhaps three months and all gummy smiles. I knew thankfully that in this day I could take a nice picture of all of us, separately and have it 'photo shopped' together to look like one. I would do that but every time I looked at it I would feel sad. We would never have that original portrait hanging above our fire as most families do. Never the memories of trying to get them washed, clean and dressed then stay that way until the cameras clicked. Funny, the kids had always just had one parent, though bizarrely it had switched during their lifetime.

I could have looked through them all day, it was already 10:30 and Sandra was leaving in a couple of hours. How I was going to cope without her I wasn't sure. She and the 'twins' had become so attached to each other. I knew she would go home and discuss with Stu, my would-be father-in-law, a move out here. Sandra promised Stu was sending me some pictures she had of Jon from home so I could compare. She said it was incredible how the next generation could look so much like the last. I held so much hope in that. Hoping they would forever resemble their dad so I would never truly loose him.

A bang on the door brought me back from a sun drenched holiday picture I had found.

"Miss Harper?" a tall uniformed man stood at the door, along with the kind officer Jenkins from Jon's disappearance day. Sandra stood behind me.

Oh god this is it, I thought. *This is closure time, they must have found his body.*

I held out my hand for Sandra to hold. This is a moment we will remember for all our lives.

"Yes?" I quivered.

"Miss Harper we have a lot of questions for you. Come with us please." and with that he took me by the arm and pulled me in the direction of his waiting patrol car.

I couldn't get any words out. I was baffled. Sandra was telling me everything would be OK and she would stay for the 'twins', forget England she was saying. I'll get Stu here. Our life is here now with you. The lady officer stayed at the house and I was driven off to god knows where. I didn't know if he could do this. I didn't know if I was under arrest or able to speak to anyone. I didn't know what this meant but as the car slowed and we pulled into his base I thought I soon might.

"The police station?" I questioned him as he opened the back seat door.

"I am not at liberty to talk madam. Not until we interview you later today."

"What...interview me for what?" I pulled my arm out of his grasp, "What is it I am supposed to have done?" I got brave.

"All in good time." he said and took me to a waiting cell-like room.

Alone in the damp, smelly waiting room I wept. Hadn't I been through enough? Forget the last few days, hadn't the last few years been reference enough to my character. I was confused and there again I saw a pair of eyes. Evil eyes that were looking directly at me. I opened mine expecting to see Andy there, but this time they were just a vision in my head. What had he said? Had they caught him? Had he blamed me? No-one knew what went on in that room except us. I knew he would try to wriggle his way out of anything. One last attempt to keep me from being happy. He had tried to take Bella out of my life before, maybe this was an attempt to take me out of hers.

It was afternoon by the time they saw me. I had clock watched, thinking Sandra would have been picking the kids up around now and facing their questions over where I had gone. We had become a good team since I had been back in their lives. We still shared a bed at night. I wasn't ready to be that alone yet.

In what I assume was an interview room I was sat down and was offered water. I took it. Anything to stem the confusion though preferably a large bottle of red which apparently wasn't on offer! The room was small considering there was to be two police officers and me in there. It was nothing like the ones in The Bill from back in Blighty. I remembered watching when I was young and trying to get out of doing my homework or going to bed.

"Miss Harper," It was a different guy "I need to tell you, you are not under arrest and all answers are up to you, *however*, should you refuse to answer anything it could look very badly should anything serious unfold."

Then I had no choice I concluded.

"To be honest, I have no clue what..." I stopped as he opened a folder and lay passport pictures down of Andy and Jon on the table that separated us. I held my hand over my mouth, I just didn't want to hear what they were going to say.

"I take it from your reaction you know these two men?"

"You know I do." I was getting angry,

"Do you mind explaining who they are please?"

"This is my husband, Andy Turner, and this," I fingered Jon's picture, he was much younger in the photo, "this is Jon Parker."

"Your lover?" asked the officer who hadn't yet spoke, his badge read Sergeant Greaves - good cop, bad cop I imagined.

"The father to my children." Who were they to pry?

"And your accomplice or did you pay him to try and murder Andy?" I looked at them blankly, "Miss Harper you were married to one of them and had a child with the other. Do you really expect that finding them both in a car crash, blood filled and knife wounds that you were not somehow involved? Please!" he lent back on his chair legs. I longed for him to fall. I remembered all the times my mum would tell me off for doing the same. Surely his pot belly and enlarged ego would be to much for those unsteady wooden legs.

"What!" I was outraged, "Don't you know what I have been through lately?"

I guessed they expected the outrage. That's

what leading questions was all about wasn't it. Getting people to spill the beans through anger.

I sat back down. "Where are they?" I asked. The folder was being opened again, he lay his hands on more pictures, blow ups this time. Would they really show me pictures of their dead bodies. I couldn't handle it if they were strangers let alone my Eskimo and his murderer.

Another officer entered in a hurry and whispered into the 'bad cops' ear.

"Interview terminated at 16:29. You're heading back downstairs Miss Harper, we'll no doubt see you again." and slammed the folder shut.

I was lead back to the waiting room, *my cell* and left over night.

They had told me nothing. Paid accomplice? My head was whirring. Was any of it true? Was it simply a new American tactic to find more details, baffling the only person left in this weird triangle relationship. But they had told me the case was closed. Nothing I was thinking was making sense. I wanted to hold my kids, I wanted Sandra to hold me and tell me everything was gong to be alright like she had so many of the nights that had past. I wanted someone anyone to get me out of this, no not someone, I wanted Jon. I wanted him more now than the day he emailed me, then the day Bella was born, than the day I saw him in the lobby of that Artic Experience, looking confused at a giant Eskimo sculpture. More than the day he pulled me out of my car after 4 years, more than the day he disappeared due to my husband, more than ever. I just wanted him here. I could pray with all my heart but he wouldn't come, he was lying in the morgue they'd said, Alone just like me.

TWENTY ONE

This letter comes to you from the grave as I store it with my will for attention of the police upon my death.

I am about to embark on a mission with fear for my own life.

I confess that these past four years my partner, Annie Harper and I have been plotting the kidnap of a man to enable us to be together.

I know this is wrong. I know this carries a sentence in prison but I love her, my Eskimo and it seems I will do anything for her.

The reason I write this is that I fear she has gone too far and I cannot get myself out. I fear upon gaining him she will ask me to go to extreme lengths to ensure he doesn't come after her again. I fear she has murderous thoughts.

If I commit this crime I have become a criminal but if I do not I think my own life is in danger.

I seek justice, to help in your case against her.

My name is Jon Parker.

Sergeant Greaves held the letter to his partner.
"Book her!" he ordered.

TWENTY TWO

"Its me, you need to get over here. Forget packing just come."

"Sandra, is everything OK? You sound panicked. God its not the 'twins' is it?"

It was late in the UK and Stu wasn't sure he was totally awake during the conversation with his wife. "What's the hurry?" he rubbed his eyes.

"The children are fine, they're with me. They've taken Annie. I don't know what's going on, I need you."

"OK, OK, calm down."

It was the first time since their sons demise that Sandra had lost her cool. She had been strong for Annie and now she was crying for him, he knew something was wrong. The phone call continued as he searched under the kitchen cupboard for his passport and fingered his keys in the door. Perhaps he should change his attire first. Pyjamas weren't really appreciated on aircraft he thought! Since Jon's death Stu had rarely got dressed. He hadn't returned to work like he was supposed to allowing Sandra instead to travel to Canada and be the supportive one. Fine he knew Annie and the kids would need support but what about him, he was hurting too. "Where's Annie gone?"

"Police turned up and took her, no-one is telling me anything."

"I'm on my way." and with that he pulled on his jeans.

Wobbling down the stairs he decided that a taxi to the airport would be better, god knows how long they would be over there and the airport car park fees could get extortionate.

Just as he picked up the phone to call it rang in his hand.

"Yes", he answered expecting it to be Sandra asking him to bring something.

"Mr Parker?" said a male voice.

"Er yes, sorry." he apologised for his rude opening, he was a respective man.

"I'm police officer Jenkins, I work with the Canadian police currently handling the case involving your son. You do know about your son Mr Parker?"

"Yes, you have been speaking with my wife as she is in the country with my sons family."

"Yes, I apologise for the time Mr Parker but we need to speak to you due to the case against Annie growing stronger and obviously you wife is living with her at present."

"Case?" he was confused, "What case? Annie, what has she supposedly done?"

"Sorry Mr I shouldn't have mentioned that. I need the next of kin for Mr Jon Parker and we still have the contact details as you, his father not Annie or his mother".

"As it happens I am coming over today but why do you need the next of kin? We've said goodbye to him. My wife can handle if there is a will officer. Unless, have you found his body?"

"Well yes Mr Parker I guess we have, only he was badly injured and it has taken a long time to get an identity."

"Surely you are not asking me to identify him? Well rather me than my wife but still...I er."

"Mr Parker I am not sure you understand," the officer cut him off, "Jon, your son, well he's alive!"

TWENTY THREE

Morning came and with it came a new interview.

"Miss Harper you do not have to say anything but if you do so it may be taken down in evidence and used against you in a court of law."

I had just been read my rights for orchestrating murder and kidnap.

I said nothing. How could I? I didn't understand what was going on. I had the idea that Andy had something to do with it and I shouldn't mention him until they did. God knows what he has said but it certainly looked like I was being blamed for his crimes.

The Sergeant pulled out two more photos. One of Andy, he lay on a slab, white and, no he wasn't framing me. He was dead!

Then Jon? His picture brought a lump to my throat. He lay peacefully. His lips so bright still on his pale face. The tears flew out of my eyes like a river running through them. I had no idea how to stop them. I was looking down at the man I had wanted my entire life, laying there never being with me again.

"Miss Harper we have a letter from Jon detailing your desire to have your husband 'taken out of the picture', *at any cost*."

I stayed silent. What letter? My mind raced. This was all far to surreal. I needed to know what was happening because this certainly wasn't a reality I wanted to live. I placed my hand on Jon's face. I still couldn't believe he was gone and now I was having to deal with the torment of being arrested. I questioned whether finding Jon and Bella again had been worthwhile. All the harm and hurt it has caused. Now he was dead, I was heartbroken, childless and facing a prison sentence. I would never regret that evening spent at his. Holding each other in arms. Him telling me about the kids growing up. My heart had mended then and there, no I wouldn't change it for the world. I know Jon would never want to leave his kids but I also knew that seeing me again one more time in his life he would have been happy.

I gave up the silence, I didn't have anymore to loose.

"What letter?"

"Mr Parker left a letter with his will detailing your desire to be with him at the cost of, he worried, murder of your husband."

"What! I wasn't with my husband and I wasn't with Jon. I hadn't seen these men, neither in four years before a little over 2 weeks ago."

The officers looked at each other.

"We are fully aware you are not going to

give in Miss Harper, our job is never that simple. Humm lets see, maybe you'll fight it was written by another?"

That was it.

"Yes it could have been written by another." I stood with my hands on the table in front of me, they didn't like that so I sat again and raised my voice, "That's exactly it, Andy. It was written by Andy. He knew where Jon lived, he knew I had moved to Canada. He knew. He killed Jon. He was in our house the day Jon disappeared!"

"Well well Miss Harper, full credit for thinking on the spot but there is one point you miss. The letter details a pet name, did you and Jon have pet names?"

"We called each other Eskimo."

"And I guess you are going to tell me that your husband knew your pet name for your lover?"

I thought hard.

No he didn't.

What was happening. I could never doubt Jon, never. There was no way he was in this to kill Andy. Yes he had said one man protecting his children is worth more than one army but he wouldn't, never, frame me.

The emails!

"Yes, the emails!"

"Pardon?"

"Andy found emails that Jon and I had sent to each other. He knew about 'Eskimo'."

They shook their heads. I was an innocent

woman fighting her corner and fighting for the right of her dead lovers name. But to them all I was was a criminal saying anything to get out of this.

There was a knock at the door and the Sergeant left.

I was left alone, alone with the picture of my dead Eskimo starring back up at me. They had found him, he could finally have a burial and a resting place, for that I had to be thankful.

The picture blurred with the water from my eyes. I didn't want to picture him like that. I swished my arms across the desk and flung the pictures across the room. Andy's turned in the air and faced Jon's on the floor. I flipped with anger. I didn't want him anywhere near him. This was all because of him. Because he was uninterested when we were married and too interested when we weren't. I ripped the picture in two, grinning. I didn't order Jon to kill Andy, I didn't kill Andy but right that second I truly could have.

The door opened on to my head as crouched down hugging Jon's picture. "Miss Harper," It was the polite lady officer from that dreadful day at my house, "Annie." she knelt down to my level. "You can leave." she said.

TWENTY FOUR

I had awoke in the middle of the night, confused and alone. I pressed the buzzer that I found in my hand and a nurse had come running. It was morning now and I saw I was hooked up to various wires and drips.

I strained to catch the eye of the nurses who were busy on shift change. I wanted to know where my well wishers were. My waking thought had been where was Annie and the 'twins'? I wanted to start our life together and though a hospital bed wasn't a good start at least we were all together, finally.

The only information the night staff were able to give me was gossip. When I first came in I was with a police escort. They thought it was because I was trying to be killed but once they found out that the guy I had come in with was dead they figured I was the bad guy.

I had taken the news of Andy demise with a huge sigh. The guy had put me through hell and back in the name of love and finally we were to be free of him. I wondered if Annie had been sad?

After all she had married him once upon a time but I figured we had a whole lifetime to talk and forget about that.

It was with sore eyes I saw my dad. It had been three and a half years since I had seen him in the flesh, since waving us off. We spoke often but since moving to the other side of the world he had not visited. He wrapped himself around me and didn't let go. He was crying. I had never seen my dad cry.

"Dad! What is it? Dad?" Why was he here alone?

"Oh son, I love you." he was kissing me and holding me.

"Dad? Please, its not Annie is it? He didn't get to her?" I tried to sit.

He cupped my face, "We thought you were dead! We all thought you were dead!"

His statement brought tears to my eyes too. "Where's Annie?"

"She's well, she's at the police station." *Complaining I* thought?

"She should be here, and mum and the kids."

"Don't try to move son. We'll get everything sorted. Everything." he wasn't making much sense, what did we have to sort?

"Mr Parker?" both me and my dad looked at him, "Mr Jon Parker?"

"Yes." I replied.

"I'm from the local police station handling this case. We have been waiting for you to wake up. Hopefully your father hasn't said too much, we asked him not too. We need a clear head from you."

"I want to see Annie Now!"

The police officer looked angrily at my dad. Was that what he wasn't supposed to tell me?

"I can understand you must be angry with her asking too much of you but…"

I cut him off, "Angry? Why am I angry? There was a mad man after us who happened to be her husband. I'm not angry at her, I want to know she is safe!" I exclaimed.

"Mr Parker, calm down, we received your letter. The letter you left in the event of your death. Its OK, we have her in custody, its all over now."

"What letter? Why would you have a letter I left in event of my death if I am still alive?"

She looked puzzled.

"I want to see her Now! Whatever you are thinking its wrong. I want to see Annie." I was struggling to sit. The muscle in my thigh was still tender from its knife mark and the bang on my head from the concrete floor ached my brain.

"Sir, could you please tell me about the letter."

"I don't know what bloody letter you are on about!" I was shouting.

"Mr Parker, you need to be very careful here. You have made a serious accusation against Miss Harper telling us she was using you to kill Mr Turner, Andy Turner, the dead guy you were found with."

"I wrote no such letter. I love Annie, we have children together. After four years of thinking she was dead we were finally going to be together. I've told you why would you have a letter I left in event of my death if I am still alive?""

The officer jumped up and spoke straight into her walkie-talkie.

"She's telling the truth sir, the letter is a fix. He's alive, why would we have a letter from the dead from a guy whose alive?"

The response down the line was audible, "SHIT!"

TWENTY FIVE

It was a grey, nameless plane that took Andy on his final journey home to England.

His sister waited confused by his stories that followed him home. A Canadian police officer had called her this morning to inform her of her brothers death. Obviously she had been worried, she hadn't heard from Andy in months. He had barely spoke to her since Annie left him and ran off with Bella years ago. He had sent her a postcard with a Canadian post mark so when the officer rang this morning she had know by his introduction and accent that it was about Andy.

She waited for his coffin to come off and would arrange a funeral. Though she would be saying goodbye to her brother she had grown up with and not the monster the police informed her he had become. She placed the plaque she had had made on top and left the pallbearers to do their job.

ANDREW PETER TURNER
35 YEARS OLD
BORN A BROTHER DIED A STRANGER

TWENTY SIX

Driving home to the 'twins' was a relief I wanted to hold them. I wanted to tell them everything was going to be alright for the rest of their lives because I would be there. Mummy was home.

I would have to tell Sandra that they had found Jon's body. She had a funeral to organise now but this time around I wanted more input. The memorial day had flown by in a wave of mourning. It was too soon I think but Sandra had used it as a way of dealing with the death of her son.

I didn't wait for the car to stop before I jumped out. The lady officer who told me I was free had driven me home. I had been offered no apology and the Sergeant that interviewed me didn't even meet my eye as I left.

I pushed open the door and saw them. Sitting together on the sofa, normally. They squealed at my presence.

"You've been shopping a long time mummy!" Jacob said

"And where are your bags?" asked Bella

I scooped them up. "I've got everything I need right here."

I spotted Sandra over in the kitchen, I mouthed 'Thank You' to her. One for holding back and letting me have my reunion and two because she had once again stepped in the limelight when I needed her help.

I didn't want to let them go, sitting them back on the sofa with a glass of milk and a Reece's Nut Bar was hard enough and I was only going into the other room!

I hugged her hello and met her eyes. "They've found him." we both said.

"I wasn't sure they'd tell you in that place." she smiled. I thought she would be pleased. A bit a closure I'm sure.

"How do you know?" I asked.

"Stu rang, he's at the hospital now. I didn't ask any questions. He flew in yesterday after I rang him. I imagine he'll be here soon. He assured me he'd packed the photos for you."

I looked at the table. The photos were still spread across as the morning I was taken. I picked up the one in the sun and one of Jon's England leavers party. There was a sadness in his eyes. I guess it wasn't long after he heard of my death. Still they're eyes looked back at me, the same from each snapshot. I blinked away tears. Would I ever be able to look at him and not cry?

Ding dong

We both looked up, I hung back, Sandra must be happy she has her support here now.

"You go love, meet your would be father in law!"

I looked in the mirror by the hall, I wasn't much of a welcome. I was exhausted and make-up less, still dressed in clothes that were two days old.

I opened the door.

I was met by his eyes. A huge blew up picture of Jon, perhaps 22 years old. He looked wonderful.

"Stu?" I began to wonder how on earth Stu had got it on the flight but...

But no, Stu was walking up the drive, then who was this?

Who was holding the photo? The photo moved and the same pair of eyes raised over the top of the canvas.

Jon, it was Jon!

I fell to my knees and cried louder than I had ever heard or felt. I heard a distant cracking of plates come from the kitchen as Sandra joined the scene.

"Jon! I didn't think you were coming home today. I was going to bring Annie up to the hospital later once I'd worked out how to tell her you... you were alive." she broke down and hugged him.

I still crouched over my knees, weeping loudly.

I felt his fingers tickle the back of my neck.

"You didn't know?"

I looked up and met his eyes. They were warm, smiling, deep and beautiful. I shook my head. It was all I could manage. He bent down to my level, struggling as I noticed he was on crutches.

"I thought you were dead!" I managed through sobs and snot!

He grunted downwards, closing his eyes as the pain got too much.

Everything went quiet. He leaned in and rubbed his nose on mine. I saw him, only him. And then I smelled him, a smell up until then had been dwindling on the pillow I was using to sleep on. His lips brushed onto mine and I was brought back to life.

I wasn't the only person in his life but right then there really was nothing else. I had stopped whaling and was smiling, perhaps for the first time since he last kissed me.

Little arms grabbed at my neck and he was pulled away from me.

"Daddy" they were shouting.

"Have you been shopping too?" Jacob made us all laugh.

I kissed the top of their heads as we all embarked on a long family hug. At last we were all together. Even Stu and Sandra had sat on the floor. I guessed it was too much for Jon to get up and I was only too happy to stay there still, together, *forever.*

Epilogue

Jon drove the last nail into the wall and I past him the large canvas. The cameras had clicked away all day and their fruition was about to hang pride of place above our fireplace, over looking the whole house. It was heavy and we had to steady it together.

Standing back we admired the way Sandra and Stu's new Canadian garden flowers had brought to life the back drop. The colours went perfectly with Bella's puffy dress and Jacobs striped waistcoat. My white gown blew slightly in the late summer breeze and Jon's suit wasn't too formal and 'groomy' as he had worried.

With a 'high-five' at our DIY success we wondered back to the 'twins'. To a monopoly board. To normality - *to life.*

About the Author

ESKIMO CALLING? IS THE FIRST NOVEL BY JODIE JONES.

HAVING A TENDENCY TO EXAGGERATE (!) JODIE USED THIS FOIBLE ALONG WITH AN APPETITE FOR IMAGINATION (DAYDREAMING!) AND PENNED HER FIRST NOVEL IN SECRET.

KNOWING ITS AN ACHIEVEMENT, JODIE HOPES IT MAKES HER LOVE ONES AS PROUD AS IT DOES HER. AN AMBITION ACHIEVED.

JODIE LIVES IN LEICESTERSHIRE WITH HER HUSBAND AND TWO CHILDREN.